SILENT MANIPULATION

Silent Manipulation

Filiz Behaettin

To my family, for your constant love, and to my readers, for sharing this journey with me.

Contents

1 Introduction — 1

2 Connections — 11

3 Unsettling Discoveries — 21

4 Obsessions — 31

5 The Spiral — 41

6 Confrontations — 49

7 The Descent — 59

8 Web of Lies — 69

9 The Unraveling — 79

10 The Final Game — 89

11 Resolutions — 99

12 New Beginnings — 107

13 Epilogue — 115

1

Introduction

"Sanity and madness. Morality and malevolence. Today, we begin exploring the thin line that separates these states. Good afternoon, everyone, and welcome to our journey into the psychology of the criminal mind."

The unconventional greeting piqued the interest of Sophia Reed, whose brilliant academic brain was already awash with ideas for her thesis on the psychology of manipulation. Lucas Hart's reputation as a highly respected professor specializing in criminal behavior was well-known worldwide and was the deciding factor for 23-year-old Sophia in choosing Harefield University to complete her graduate degree. Professor Hart's psychological insight and provocative theories intrigued her, and she was impressed by his charismatic command of the room. She was satisfied that she had chosen wisely.

She listened with a growing fascination as Professor Hart began his lecture. Although his approach was rumored to be unorthodox, his results spoke for themselves and contributed to Harefield University having one of the most prestigious psychology faculties in the state. Hart's confident and powerful voice resonated through the hall as he addressed his captive audience, each student seemingly held in thrall by his commanding presence.

"I'm sure many of you have seen the recent television documentary about the case of a local man, Charles Edmund. In fact, Charles grew up here in Harefield, not too far from this university. As a child, he was known to have exhibited signs of high intelligence but lacked empathy toward others. He could be charming, but this was often used as a manipulation technique, as was soon discovered by his teachers. By the time he had reached fifteen years of age, Charles was already known to the authorities for his involvement in a spate of minor thefts. However, his charismatic persona ensured the punishments he received were often on the lenient side.

"During his teenage years, Charles—like many of us here, I suspect—developed a fascination with crime novels, especially psychological thrillers." At this point, Hart's deep-set, piercing blue eyes scanned the lecture theater. Sophia could have sworn that they briefly locked with her own , and she felt a jolt of electricity course through her body. *Why would he single me out?* Or perhaps it was the unexpected way her body reacted to him? Incapable of holding Hart's gaze, Sophia quickly looked away from the professor's intimidating and mesmerizing stare, convincing herself that she must be mistaken. *There's a ton of students in here. Why would he be drawn to me?* Sophia was a striking woman, but she played down her appearance and had always been unaware of her understated, natural beauty. Today, as she often did, she had scrunched her long, wavy, chestnut brown hair into a messy bun, which perfectly complemented her comfortable attire of a beige turtleneck and black jeans. She wore no makeup aside from a sweep of black mascara on the already thick, dark lashes that framed her clear, green eyes. A thin layer of powder constituted a futile attempt to diminish the light splatter of freckles across her nose and cheeks that she had hated as a child. Realizing that Hart's perceived attention had caused her mind to wonder, she quickly forced her attention back to his lecture.

Professor Hart had moved on. "Charles is documented to have frequently boasted about his manipulation skills and the power it gave him over others," he was saying. "He enjoyed playing mind games with his peers. As a teenager, his academic performance remained stellar. However, his social interactions were based on a dangerous pattern of deceit and control.

"When he was twenty-two, Charles left Harefield and moved to the city to pursue a career in finance. By this stage, he had learned to use his charm and intelligence to his advantage, quickly landing him a high-paying job. Almost unsurprisingly, given his behavior pattern, he soon used his position to embezzle funds from the company that employed him. Over the next five years, he managed to siphon millions of dollars from the company while maintaining the façade of a dedicated employee. Now, I'll ask you to turn your attention to the screen."

The vast screen at the front of the lecture theater flickered into life as Professor Hart loaded a presentation from his laptop.

"Let's look at the manipulation tactics used by Charles to avoid detection for all that time," he invited. "Firstly, we have charm and flattery. Charles often flattered his colleagues and especially his superiors. This led to him being low on their list of suspects whenever something untoward occurred."

Hart clicked on the next slide. "Then we have the buzzword of the moment—gaslighting. Whenever his discrepancies were noticed, Charles would manipulate the facts so that others would start to doubt their perceptions."

The next slide materialized on the screen.

"Finally, we have isolation," Professor Hart continued. "Charles Edmund was able to identify potential whistleblowers and isolate them by spreading rumors about them or creating conflict between them and their co-workers."

Another slide filled the screen.

"Edmund's downfall began when a female junior employee, whom we'll call Jane, noticed irregularities in the accounts. Unlike her colleagues, Jane seemed immune to Edmund's charm. She began meticulously gathering evidence that she then presented to the authorities. Charles was arrested and charged. During his subsequent trial, his manipulative tactics were laid bare to the jury. He received a twenty-five-year jail term."

Professor Hart clicked on the next slide. "While he was awaiting trial, Charles was analyzed by a team of psychologists who noted several traits consistent with psychopathy, the first of which was a lack of empathy. Charles showed no remorse for his actions. To him, his victims were merely pawns in his game. He also exhibited narcissism, demonstrated by the fact that he had an inflated sense of self-importance, so much so that the prospect of being caught never troubled him as he believed he was above the law. Finally, his superficial charm was undeniable, giving him the unparalleled ability to manipulate. Therefore, deception came easily to him."

The next slide appeared. "This case study illustrates several psychological theories that we'll examine in finer detail. Edmund's lack of empathy and manipulative nature are classic signs of psychopathy, which—as most of you will know—often correlates with criminal behavior. His use of charm, gaslighting, and isolation are common tactics that manipulative individuals employ to control and deceive. Edmund's case clearly demonstrates how high intelligence can sometimes enable more sophisticated and prolonged criminal activities than we would otherwise see.

"So, we can conclude from this," he said as another slide illuminated the screen, "that the case of Charles Edmund is a compelling example of how intelligence combined with psychopathic traits can lead to an advanced level of criminal behavior. Hopefully, however, it also highlights the importance of vigilance and integrity in detecting and preventing manipulation so that individuals engaging in this kind of activity can be caught and stopped."

As Professor Hart went on to discuss the interplay between criminal behavior and psychological manipulation, Sophia found her mind wandering again. She had already studied this topic at length as part of her undergraduate degree. Instead, she found herself studying the alluring figure of Professor Lucas Hart. He was obviously much older than her—in his mid-40s, she suspected from the touch of silver at the temples of his dark hair—but aside from his illustrious career at the university, she knew very little about him. Like her fellow students, she had scoured Google, Wikipedia, and the university website for information on her tutors to help her choose the best mentor for her thesis. Most of the faculty staff had bios that listed their families and their hobbies as well as their academic achievements, but under Lucas Hart, those sections were frustratingly blank. Undoubtedly, he was highly respected in his field, but Sophia sensed an air of mystery surrounding him that acted like a magnet field, pulling her toward him.

Everything about Hart indicated a strong connection to the world of academia, from his neatly styled hair to his well-tailored suit. Even his sleek reading glasses seemed to add to his intellectual charm. He had a healthy complexion with unblemished skin, aside from a few faint lines around his eyes and mouth that hinted at both his age and a lifetime of experiences. He was tall, Sophia guessed at around six feet one, with a well-maintained physique that suggested he kept himself fit. His broad shoulders added to his commanding presence and made it impossible for him not to draw attention when he entered a room. He had a strong, chiseled jaw-line, with slight stubble being the only feature that suggested anything other than polish and refinement.

Sophia decided that the two most suitable adjectives for Professor Lucas Hart were *sophistication* and *mystery*. He had already gained her respect through his reputation, and hearing him lecture on his specialist subject further convinced her that his sharp mind matched his refined looks. She had often heard his methods described as controversial, but sitting in his lecture theater had only increased her intrigue and desire to discover more about him. It also alarmed her that she found him dangerously attractive. It was an unusual response for Sophia, who had trained her brilliant mind to guard her emotions with a fortress of logic. However, perhaps the fortress was not as impenetrable as she had imagined.

Turning her attention back to the lecture, Sophia heard Professor Hart discussing some of his notorious theories on the criminal mind. "While the Dark Triad of narcissism, Machiavellianism, and psychopathy is a well-known concept," he was saying, "I invite you to open your mind to the idea that individuals high in these traits can manipulate others by creating a 'dark charisma.' This dark charisma has been described as an almost magnetic attraction that draws people in, making them more susceptible to manipulation. The theory suggests that certain people possess an innate ability to project this dark charisma, making their manipulative tactics more effective."

Sophia sat up straighter in her seat. This was the exact subject that she wanted to study for her thesis. Professor Hart's papers on the Dark Triad Influence were widely revered, but his opinions on dark charisma were dismissed by many in the academic world as conspiracy theories, and, therefore, she had not expected them to come up in a lecture, especially this early in the semester! *Perhaps it's a sign I should ask him to mentor me?* His reputation and intimidating persona meant she would need to find the courage to approach him. She stifled a sigh and tried not to contemplate how the scene would play out. Although she projected an air of quiet strength and determination, Sophia's mind sometimes betrayed her by being over-analytical, which sometimes led to bouts of social anxiety and self-doubt. Her slender and petite five feet four-inch physique added to her insecurities. Just the thought of entering the personal space of the charming but mysterious professor was daunting. Still, despite her mild and slightly serious demeanor, Sophia had a core of steely determination. If Professor Hart were the right person to mentor her through her thesis, she would not let the opportunity pass her by.

Professor Hart was now concluding his lecture. "The concept of the Dark Triad Influence offers a nuanced understanding of how certain personality traits, such as the ones exhibited by Charles Edmund, can lead to manipulative behavior," he stated. "Individuals and organizations can better protect themselves from potential harm by recognizing these traits and their associated tactics. I hope this introduction has whet your appetite for the psychological explorations that will follow in the coming weeks." He gave an enigmatic smile. "I look forward to addressing you all again soon."

The room emptied slowly, with students lingering to discuss the lecture with one another or, it seemed to Sophia, simply to bask in Professor Hart's charismatic presence. It was frustrating for Sophia, whose excitement and fear were building. She needed to approach him before she lost her nerve. What she didn't need, however, was an audience. Still, she was now 100 percent certain that she had to speak with Lucas Hart to seek at least his guidance, if not his mentorship. She eventually garnered enough courage to approach the lectern, where he was shutting down his laptop.

"Professor Hart," Sophia began, keeping her voice steady despite the nervous flutter in her stomach. "Thank you for that lecture; I found it incredibly insightful. My name is Sophia Reed. I'm a grad student, and I'm writing my thesis about the psychology of manipulation. I want to challenge the existing theories on manipulation and control and take them further. Your work is very much in alignment with my thoughts on the subject. I'd be grateful if you could spare some time to discuss some of my ideas and, ideally, consider if you'd be willing to mentor me."

The professor looked up from his laptop, and the intensity in his icy blue eyes caused Sophia's breath to hitch. There was a brief silence as he studied her with a gaze that could penetrate into the depths of the soul. Finally, he spoke. "Sophia Reed," he murmured, a slow smile spreading across his face. "Well, well. Yes, I know who you are. Your reputation precedes you, my dear. Your undergraduate dissertation caused quite a stir. It won you the highest grade in the state, didn't it? So, you've chosen to write about the Dark Triad Influence for your thesis?"

"Yes," replied Sophia. "And how the theory can be applied to the psychology of manipulation."

Hart nodded slowly, his eyes never leaving her face. "It would be foolish of me to ignore such a request from a student as promising as yourself. I'd be most happy to discuss your theory with a view to becoming your mentor. I have a feeling that the situation may be mutually advantageous. I'm free tomorrow afternoon. Come by my office at three o'clock, and we'll talk in more depth."

Sophia felt exhilarated despite the professor's imperious tone. "Thank you, Professor Hart. I'll be there."

Hart nodded before gathering up his laptop and sweeping majestically from the lecture theater.

Sophia's anticipation intensified as she realized she was a step closer to being mentored by one of the most respected academics in the field. But she also felt something else, something that wasn't as easy to label. She sensed that she was on the cusp of something significant, but couldn't yet identify what it was. Sophia's logical brain was unused to dealing with such abstract concepts, and she found the experience unnerving.

She contemplated this as she exited Emerson Hall, where the psychology faculty was based, and crossed the courtyard to the main university building where her next lecture was held. Realizing she had a few minutes to spare, she sat down on a wooden bench and watched the breeze rustling through the ivy that clung to the stone walls of the old building. She was still sure that she wanted Professor Hart to be her mentor, but after meeting him in person, she was forced to admit that she was excited by more than just his academic prowess. She found him attractive, but it was more than that. There was an air of mystery surrounding him and even a hint of danger. Shaking her head, Sophia reprimanded herself for letting her imagination run riot. She made a valiant effort to regain her focus, hoping she wouldn't be so distracted at their next meeting.

2

Connections

Sophia spent most of the following morning alternating between making herself see reason and trying to calm her nerves. Her thesis was the culmination of her work so far, the work that was her life's greatest passion. Therefore, she couldn't allow herself to be distracted by something as trivial and clichéd as a handsome professor. Lucas Hart was the leader in his academic field and deserved far better than her objectification. She needed to cast her personal feelings aside so as not to endanger the chances of him deciding to mentor her. There was too much riding on this.

Her morning lectures passed in a blur, and at three o'clock precisely, Sophia found herself knocking on Professor Hart's office door.

"Come in."

Sophia's breath caught in her throat as she entered the office, which appeared exactly as she had imagined. Two of the walls were completely lined with bookshelves, each crammed with volumes that were mainly psychology-related but a few on other subjects as well. The modestly sized room was dominated by a large, antique desk at the center, behind which sat the imposing figure of the professor with his fingers steepled as he watched her approach.

"Ms. Reed," he greeted her smoothly, with his voice every bit as commanding as it had been in the lecture theater the previous day. "How delightful to see you. Please take a seat."

Sophia took a deep breath and sat in the chair he gestured toward, smoothing down her dark blue jeans and straightening her tailored blazer as she did so. "Thank you, Professor Hart," she said as she sat. "I can't tell you how much I appreciate you taking the time to discuss my thesis."

Hart's lips curved into his enigmatic smile. "The pleasure is all mine. It's an honor to be asked to mentor such a promising student. Besides, how could I resist when the subject matter is so close to my heart?"

Sophia felt a shiver run down her spine at his words. Had she imagined it, or had the way he said "close to my heart" have an almost... intimate quality? She blinked rapidly several times to clear her head. This was precisely what she was afraid of. She needed to remain focused on the task at hand—trying to regain the professor's mentorship.

As if he sensed her discomfort, Hart's demeanor changed, and he appeared to relax. He sat back in his chair and placed both hands in the pockets of his trousers, making him appear more receptive. "I'd be more than happy to mentor you through your thesis, Sophia," he said, "Please, tell me what ideas you've had so far."

As she warmed to her favorite subject, Sophia found the conversation flowed easily between them. Hart had a wealth of knowledge on the psychology of manipulation and seemed impressed by her level of understanding. His insights into her research were invaluable, and she was drawn to his enthusiasm for the subject. His gentle encouragement enabled her to discuss her ideas freely, and she soon felt a rapport building between them. Their intellectual chemistry was undeniable, making it perfectly sensible that they should collaborate. However, Sophia couldn't help but sense an undercurrent to their interaction, a lingering tension that she couldn't quite fathom. Nevertheless, she was determined not to let it interfere with their work, so she cast it aside and tried her best to concentrate on her thesis.

As they worked together through those first few weeks of the semester, Sophia felt a deep connection forming between her and her mentor. The long hours they spent poring over case studies and psychological theories brought them closer as they bounced ideas off each other and playfully debated each new theory. Hart's intensity and infectious enthusiasm intoxicated Sophia. However, the more their relationship grew, so did her sense of unease, and each day, she found it just a bit harder to ignore.

Their afternoon sessions often ran into the evening. One evening, as they were wrapping up, Hart leaned back on his chair in a similar fashion to their first meeting and turned to Sophia with a contemplative look. "Have you ever considered the darker aspects of manipulation? I know we've discussed how it can be used to influence. But what about control? Have you ever considered the implications?"

Sophia heard faint alarm bells going off at his abrupt change of tone, but she shook her head to silence them. *This is a teaching session, not a date*! She hesitated before replying.

"Of course, I have, Professor," she answered eventually. "Manipulation has proven to be a dangerous tool in the wrong hands."

Hart seemed amused by her answer. "Please, Sophia, call me Lucas. I think we've gotten to know each other well enough now to drop the formalities. Manipulation is a fascinating topic, isn't it? I mean, it gives us the power to bend someone's will to our own. The power to make them dance to our tune."

The tension between them seemed to have risen by a notch. The prospect of dropping formalities with Lucas Hart thrilled Sophia and chilled her simultaneously. She forced a smile while she tried to process the influx of thoughts whirling through her mind. "That's an... interesting theory, Lucas," she hesitantly replied, "but also terrifying."

Hart gave Sophia a broad smile, his eyes gleaming in the dimming light. She felt like a rabbit trapped in the headlights of his almost predatory gaze. "Fear is a powerful motivator, Sophia. Remember that."

Then his tone changed again, and the tension levels dropped once more as they discussed when they would meet the following day. But as Sophia left his office that night, she couldn't shake the feeling that Lucas Hart had hidden depths she hadn't yet uncovered. Her growing attraction to him made impartiality difficult. And she suspected that his fascination with manipulation and intense interest in her and her research was suggesting that he also saw their relationship as more than just mentor/student. However, she was too unsure of herself to act upon it. All she knew was that it was starting to feel... too personal. Too close for comfort.

***

The following day, the Harefield University campus was awash with devastating news. A woman in her twenties had been brutally murdered in the heart of the city the previous night. The news channels had tried to play down the gruesome nature of the murder. Yet, there were aspects of the crime scene that were eerily reminiscent of the last case study Professor Hart had used in his criminal psychology lectures, and which he and Sophia had further dissected in one of their recent sessions.

The similarities were enough to make Sophia's blood run cold as she watched the report on the morning news. The perpetrator had apparently left no evidence at the scene, and detectives had no leads as to who had committed the heinous crime.

Sophia's mind raced as she walked to Emerson Hall for her next meeting with Lucas. Her thoughts had become fixated on the murder, exacerbated by Hart's unsettling behavior the previous day. She wanted to discuss the crime with him in case it would be beneficial to her thesis, but there was a nagging voice in the back of her mind that she couldn't silence, warning her to remain vigilant and alert to the presence of danger.

Lucas was waiting for her in his office, his laptop already loaded with a rolling news feed. He watched her as she entered the room, his expression unreadable. "Sophia. I suppose you've heard what happened?"

She nodded her response. "I have, yes. It's horrific."

Hart studied her face intently. "I believe it may be the ultimate example of manipulation. If so, don't you think it would be the perfect case study for your thesis?"

Sophia frowned, unable to accept what she had just heard. She tried to keep her voice steady when she replied. "A terrifying murder has been committed, Lucas. Do you really think we should exploit the victim and her family by detailing her death in my thesis so soon after it occurred?"

Hart removed his reading glasses, and his bright blue eyes darkened, momentarily flickering with an emotion Sophia didn't recognize but felt to be dangerous. "Perhaps," he retorted, "or maybe it's what the perpetrator intends you to do. You can't have missed the similarities between the murder and the cases we've been discussing. Have you considered that they may have been inspired by the same fascinating concepts we've covered? And if so, can you really pass up this opportunity to examine the case?"

Sophia's heart was pounding so hard that she felt her chest might explode. Everything was swimming in her head, and, for once, she couldn't get a grip on the situation. *Was Lucas Hart really so callous that he wants me to become embroiled in a murder that happened practically on the doorstep, just to enhance my thesis? Or does he know something that I don't? Is there a connection between this murder and our work that he wants me to discover?* Sophia was overwhelmed and felt a sudden urge to be out in the fresh air, clearing her head. "I… I need to give this some thought, Lucas," she stammered. "Excuse me," she added, and she turned around, rushing out through his office door.

Hart said nothing but just watched her leave with an inscrutable expression. Once outside his office, Sophia couldn't erase the thought of those piercing blue eyes following her every move. She kept checking over her shoulder as she hurried down the hallway, fearful that she was being watched. Only when she reached the relative safety of the crowded courtyard did she allow herself to stop and contemplate what had just happened. Lucas Hart had gone out of his way to lead her research down a particular path, and now a murder had been committed in the vicinity of the university using the exact tactics that he was encouraging her to study. *Is it a coincidence, or something more?* Sophia was astute enough to realize that the boundaries of their relationship were blurring, which altered her usually accurate perception. But his words and actions still gave her cause for concern.

It had been a long time since anyone had awakened feelings in Sophia the way Lucas Hart was doing, and it made her feel vulnerable. But she was delighted with how her thesis was coming along and didn't want to do anything that might jeopardize it. But she needed to put her mind at rest over Hart. Therefore, she decided to do some research on her own to discover more about him. *What's happened in his past that he needs to keep so private? What makes him tick?* She didn't know what it could be, but she was almost certain that he was keeping something from her. *Why else is there so little about his personal life online?* She was determined to uncover the truth.

As soon as she got home, she began trawling the internet but was disappointed that her searches revealed little more than she already knew. Instead, she found herself falling down a research rabbit hole instigated by her search for information on Dark Triad Influence. There were articles written by Professor Hart himself, which had inspired further discussions. Her attention was constantly drawn back to one notorious paper written by Hart called *Dark Charisma: The Synergy of the Dark Triad*, which was the paper Hart cited in the first of his lectures that Sophia attended. It was a theory that Sophia was already familiar with, but now she felt compelled to reread it:

> When the traits of narcissism, Machiavellianism, and psychopathy converge in an individual, they can create a concept that some refer to as "dark charisma."

Sophia could almost hear Hart's charismatic voice reading the words aloud to her. She continued:

> This dark charisma is a potent blend of charm, strategic thinking, and emotional detachment, enabling these individuals to become exceptionally effective manipulators. Dark charisma operates as follows:

1. **Attractiveness and Persuasiveness.** The narcissistic charm makes them attractive and persuasive, drawing people in and gaining their trust.

2. **Strategic Manipulation.** Machiavellian traits enable them to plan and execute manipulative strategies with precision, often going unnoticed.

3. **Emotional Ruthlessness.** Psychopathic traits allow them to manipulate without remorse, making them more willing to engage in unethical or harmful behaviors to achieve their goals.

Sophia found her thoughts drifting back to Jamie, her high school boyfriend. Jamie was one of the popular kids, the football team's quarterback and Sophia had been astonished when he showed an interest in her. It wasn't that she was unattractive; she'd been striking even in her teenage years. However, she'd always put schoolwork first and dressed nothing like the flashy, confident girls that Jamie usually hung out with. She'd been flattered but wary when Jamie first started showering her with attention, but he was persistent and eventually wore her down. He overwhelmed her with affection (which she later discovered was a common tactic known as "love bombing"), and she fell for him hook, line, and sinker. He had been the center of her world. For the first time in her life, she had found something more important than studying. Although her grades didn't slip too badly, she was occasionally late for classes or missed assignment deadlines—all unheard of in her pre-Jamie era.

Eventually, Sophia became aware of subtle changes in Jamie's attitude toward her. Whereas he'd previously been nothing but attentive, she noticed that he started criticizing her in front of their friends, often about how she wore her hair, the way she dressed, her lack of makeup, and so on. She didn't think much about it at first, but it became more frequent and caustic, sometimes causing an awkward atmosphere. It eventually reached a stage where their friends were reluctant to be around them. Jamie started being late for dates and often didn't show up at all, with no apologies or excuses. Sophia felt more devalued and discarded as time went on until it reached a stage where her family and friends felt like they needed to stage an intervention.

Initially, Sophia had refused to acknowledge that Jamie was anything less than perfect. It took her walking in on him making out with the head cheerleader to see the truth and end the relationship. But it broke her, with devastating consequences. She eventually emerged on the other side, but as a different person. Gone was the carefree girl with the sunny nature. What remained was an emotionally guarded woman who wouldn't let anything distract her from the most important goal in her life: her education. Until she met Lucas Hart.

In a moment of clarity, Sophia saw parallels between Jamie's actions and Professor Hart's. Jamie had pulled Sophia into his world with attention and flattery. Hadn't Hart done precisely the same thing by constantly praising her academic achievements? Jamie had occupied all her time, making her feel like the most important person in his life and isolating her from her family and friends. *How often have I been out with friends since Lucas began mentoring me? How frequently have I called or visited my family?*

The more Sophia studied Hart's theories about manipulation, the more she saw traces of it in her life and his. Hart was a master of his craft, and Sophia suddenly feared that she could be his latest subject rather than his student. She resolved to uncover the truth before it slipped beyond her reach.

3

Unsettling Discoveries

Sophia awoke the following morning from an unsatisfactory sleep, in which her dark suspicions about the murder and her growing attraction to Professor Hart had become entangled in her dreams. She walked to her morning lectures on the university campus, thinking the fresh air may do her some good. But not even the crisp morning air could help her unravel the tangle of suspicions circling in her mind. Nor did the bustling crowd of students in the grounds provide a distraction. Murders, especially such gruesome ones, were fortunately few in the area, so it was unsurprising that the news should shake her. However, her persistent hunch that Professor Hart could be involved formed the lion's share of her discomfort. There were too many coincidences. Lucas was obviously fascinated by the theory of manipulation—after all, he had made an illustrious career from studying it! *But what about his intense interest in my research and his strange behavior the other day? It all seems too coincidental.* Sophia did not usually indulge in speculation, especially unsupported by fact, but in this case, she had a gut feeling that was too strong to ignore.

By the time she reached Emerson Hall, she had made a decision. Her sanity, not to mention her future, was at stake if she continued

21

to have sleepless nights. It was a risk she couldn't afford to take. Therefore, she decided to be proactive before she reached breaking point. *I'll conduct my own inquiries into the murder.* She could use Lucas's techniques – after all, she had learned from the master himself! If nothing else became of it, she could use the research for her thesis, but the best-case scenario would be that she would put her mind at rest regarding Professor Hart's involvement. Yes, it was a dangerous game to play, but so was being in such close proximity to a suspected murderer. Sophia felt as though she had no choice.

Her first stop was the university library, where she pored over the wealth of online articles about the murder. Details were in scarce supply, but she eventually managed to piece together a timeline of the victim's last hours from what had been reported. The unfortunate victim was a young woman named Emily Warren. The last sighting of her alive had been on CCTV, which showed her leaving a local bar with an unnamed man. Her body was found in an alleyway the following morning. So far, the police still had no new leads, and there was growing concern that the case would grow cold unless more evidence was discovered. Quickly.

When Sophia had gleaned all the information she could about the murder from the internet, she moved on to digging into Lucas Hart's background. She spent hours in the library's archives, trawling for any information she could find. Hart was a respected figure in the field of psychology and had a renowned career. Therefore, he had numerous publications and accolades to his name. Most of the articles pertaining to him were highly complimentary, but there was a thread running through many others that hinted at controversy, especially the blurring of ethical boundaries in the pursuit of knowledge.

Several hours later, Sophia was on the verge of giving up when she stumbled upon an old microfiche newspaper article that caught her eye. Apparently, there had been a whiff of scandal at the university where Hart lectured before coming to Harefield. It had obviously been well covered up, as Sophia had not seen it mentioned in any of the other articles she had perused that morning. She wondered if all references to the incident had been removed from the Harefield faculty library. *Was this one accidentally missed? Was it deliberate?*

As Sophia continued to read the article, she discovered that Hart had been accused of manipulating a female student into taking part in a psychological experiment without her consent. There had been enough evidence for the student to take the case to court, but she seemed to have accepted a settlement before things got that far. There was no proof that linked Hart to any wrongdoing, and he was quietly transferred to Harefield. Sophia didn't know if the pounding of her heart from what she'd discovered or lack of sleep was making her feel so light-headed, but even in that state, she realized that she had uncovered something significant.

Pieces of the puzzle were falling into place, but she was far from getting the whole picture. However, the more she learned, the stronger her gut feeling grew that Hart was somehow connected to Emily Warren's murder. But all she had were her suspicions, and they were no good to her without concrete proof. There was no doubt in her mind that Hart was capable of the level of manipulation required to orchestrate such a murder—the unproven allegations of the student at his previous university were testament to that. But what Sophia didn't understand was why the man she was undeniably developing feelings for would do such a thing in the first place. *What motive could he possibly have?*

Sophia spent the rest of the day following up her investigations, trying to unlock more clues with little success. When it reached the evening, she decided to call it a day. She had scarcely exited the library when she felt a presence looming behind her. Sophia felt the hairs on the back of her neck rise, and her stomach started doing somersaults. Steeling herself, she turned around to confront her pursuer. She found herself looking at Professor Hart, standing as still as a statue with an unreadable expression on his face.

"Sophia," he greeted her in the calm and friendly manner she had become accustomed to. "You missed my lecture today. That's highly out of character for you. I was concerned that you may have taken ill, but some of the other students informed me that you'd been in the library all day. Were you looking for something in particular? I hope all is well."

Sophia felt as though guilt must be etched on her face, but she forced herself to remain calm, using relaxation techniques she had learned in the aftermath of her breakup with Jamie. "I was just doing some research for my thesis, Lucas," she replied. She nearly buckled under Hart's gaze as she felt his eyes pierce through to her soul.

"As commendable as that is," he said, "I feel I would be failing in my duties as your mentor if I didn't issue a warning."

Sophia's eyebrows shot up in inquiry, and Hart's tone hardened. "Be careful, Sophia," he continued. "Sometimes the answers we seek can lead us down a very dark path."

Sophia struggled to find the saliva she needed to moisten her dry throat. She resorted to nodding. "Understood," she croaked, "and thank you for the advice. It's appreciated."

Hart's demeanor shifted again, and he beamed at her. "Good," he said, "I look forward to seeing you at our mentoring session tomorrow. Don't be late!" And with that, he swept off.

Sophia watched Lucas retreat down the corridor and into his office before she turned and walked away. Although she knew it was impossible, she felt his eyes still followed her every move. *Why does he affect me so much?* Sophia sighed to herself, knowing that her growing feelings for him made her vulnerable, especially if what she suspected about him held even a hint of truth. From now on, she needed to be on her guard. If he was playing a game, then she was his unwitting pawn. But there was no way she'd be taken without a fight.

Sophia decided to suspend her investigations over the next few days to prevent Hart from becoming suspicious. Despite her misgivings, she continued to attend his lectures and their mentoring meetings. However, to her dismay, his behavior at their sessions seemed to become increasingly erratic. He would drop hints and make cryptic comments that unsettlingly and disorientingly affected her, sometimes leaving her doubting the credibility of her own perceptions. Her thesis, however, was coming along brilliantly, and she was loathe to do anything to stem the flow of creativity.

After one particularly intense session, where they had worked on her thesis from lunchtime into the evening, Hart suddenly leaned in close to Sophia.

"Do you ever feel like someone is watching you, Sophia?" His voice was so low, it was barely a whisper. "Like you're being followed."

Sophia jumped away from him in alarm. The truth was that, yes, those were the exact sensations she had experienced ever since he caught her coming out of the library. *How could he possibly know that?* She forced a smile. "Why do you ask, Lucas?"

Hart returned her smile, but there was no warmth in his eyes. "It's just a thought. Sometimes, our minds play tricks on us, you know? Make us see things that aren't there. But, of course, you know that already."

Sophia kept smiling, but her fear was increasing. She was sure Hart was toying with her, trying to make her doubt herself. But why would he bother? Had he worked out that she suspected him of being involved in the murder? Whatever his game, it was vital that she stayed strong and kept the upper hand. She needed her wits about her if she was going to grapple with a brilliant psychological mind like Hart's.

Despite her best intentions, Sophia found it impossible to fall asleep again that night. Although she knew that adequate sleep was crucial to her well-being, she couldn't quell the tempest brewing in her mind. *This can't go on.* If she wanted to link Hart to the murder, then she needed to find concrete evidence, or else she would need to let the matter drop. But Sophia's previous experiences had fortified her inner strength, and her clever, inquiring mind wouldn't allow her to quit. Just as she was finally falling asleep, inspiration struck her with a flash, and her eyes flew open. *Of course, his office will have answers!* She knew that Lucas kept meticulous notes on every case he'd ever worked on in that majestic desk and the filing cabinets that lined one wall of the office. His entire life's work was documented within that room. *If there's anything remotely incriminating, it will be in there.*

Hart had a faculty meeting the following day. She knew this, as they had discussed it while scheduling their next mentoring session. Although it only opened a small window of opportunity, she was determined to use it to make her move. Therefore, she found herself slipping into his office in the morning, grateful that he never locked the door. In Sophia's mind, leaving the door unlocked didn't mean that Lucas Hart had nothing to hide. It simply meant he was confident that no one would go looking.

The office was eerily quiet when she entered, so much so that it was hard to distinguish the sound of her heart pounding in her chest from the ticking of the grandfather clock in the corner. She approached Hart's desk, sifting through the papers and files strewn carelessly across the top. They contained nothing of immediate interest, just as Sophia expected. Hart was a highly intelligent man; there was no way he'd leave a trail of his misdemeanors on display like that. The desk had several drawers, the first of which she tried with a trembling hand. She was almost incredulous when it slid open. The arrogance of the man! Did he honestly think he was so far above suspicion that locking his drawers was unnecessary? The drawer was a deep one and contained a stack of notebooks, each one filled to the brim with Lucas Hart's neat, precise handwriting. Flipping through them, she realized they were detailed accounts of his various psychological experiments, case studies, and personal observations.

The drawer underneath held exactly the same content, as did the one below that. But it was only while exploring that third drawer, Sophia found anything relevant—a notebook with the initials EW scrawled on the cover. She released a breath she was unaware she'd been holding as she opened it and scanned the pages. The notebook contained details of Hart's interactions with the "subject," including observations on behavior and a psychological profile. The final entry was dated the night of the murder.

Sophia could hardly bring herself to read that final entry. According to notes, Hart had been studying the "subject" closely, manipulating and pushing them to their limits. However, he was careful not to mention anything that may help identify them, such as age or gender. The nature of the experiment was shocking in itself and undoubtedly exceeded the boundaries of morality and ethics. But it was the note written in the margin that chilled Sophia's heart—"Experiment concluded."

It took Sophia a moment to realize why the notebook was becoming so difficult to read, and then she noticed that her hands were shaking violently. This was it; this was her proof. *So why, then, do I feel anything but triumphant?* With a sinking heart, she admitted to herself that the only course of action open to her was to hand the notebook to the police and allow them to conclude whether or not Hart was responsible for Emily Warren's murder. It was her duty to expose him whether she wanted to or not. She pocketed the notebook and turned to leave, but the door creaked open before she could do so, and Hart stood in the doorway.

"Sophia, what a pleasant surprise. I didn't expect to find you in here. I thought you knew I had a meeting." His words were friendly enough, but his tone was anything but.

Sophia's mind raced, searching for a plausible excuse why she should be in his office. "Sorry, Lucas," she said. "I couldn't find some of my thesis notes and thought I may have left them in here. I didn't mean to intrude, but I do need them quite urgently."

Hart's expression remained unaltered. "Oh, I see," he countered. "And there was I, thinking you'd been digging again despite my warning. Determined to undercover whatever dark secrets I've been hiding." His eyes never strayed from hers, and electricity crackled between them.

Sophia stepped back, grateful the purloined notebook was hidden in her pocket. She laughed nervously. "Of course not," she managed, albeit unconvincingly. "Sorry, Lucas, but I've really got to go. I'll catch up with you soon."

"Oh, I don't think you're going anywhere," he said mildly, his eyes gleaming with an ominous light.

Sophia said nothing, hypnotized by his gaze.

Hart stepped forward, his smile gone and his voice low and menacing. "Be careful, Sophia. You're playing a dangerous game."

Sophia gasped, partly from fear and partly from the exhilaration of Hart's close proximity. As quick as lightning, he reached out and seized her wrist. Sophia froze.

But then Hart laughed, and Sophia once again had no idea if the danger she sensed was real or a figment of her over-active imagination.

4

Obsessions

Sophia sat in her small apartment that evening, replaying the events from earlier in the day. For one terrifying moment, she had honestly thought that Hart knew what she had discovered and meant to harm her. Even when he laughed, he hadn't released her wrist, and Sophia had visions of him taking her hostage or, worst-case scenario, her not leaving his office alive. But what scared her the most was the excitement she felt at his touch. This was the man she suspected of being involved in a brutal murder, so why was she so attracted to him? Her cheeks flamed as she recalled the electricity that flowed between them, even when she believed he would take her hostage.

Hart had laughed again before releasing his grip on her wrist. "Gosh, Sophia," he said, "your face is a picture. Surely you didn't think I was being serious? Anyone would think you had a guilty conscience or something!" He laughed again.

Sophia had swallowed, unable to ascertain whether she felt relief that she was unharmed or disappointment that their physical contact had been broken. She was confused; her common sense warned her to put as much distance as possible between herself

31

and this man. But her body betrayed her by sending her powerful messages to do just the opposite.

After he had released his grip on her wrist, the mood had lightened dramatically. Hart chatted freely with her about the meeting he had just left and his new ideas for her thesis. She was just about to leave when he asked her, "So, did you find them?"

She was puzzled for a second before realizing he meant the fictitious notes she was supposed to have been looking for. "Oh, no," she answered. "They weren't on your desk where I thought I'd left them. They must be in my apartment somewhere. I'll have another look when I get back."

"Oh, okay." A frown momentarily crossed his face. "I thought I saw you put something in your pocket. My mistake."

Sophia's heart was beating so loudly that she was sure Lucas would hear it. Unable to speak, she threw a quick smile in his direction before scuttling out of the office. If her actions surprised Hart, he didn't show it. "We haven't arranged a time for our next meeting," he had called down the corridor after. "I'll text you."

Now, back in her apartment, Sophia sat with the stolen notebook in front of her. Her body was motionless, contrasting with her mind, which was awash with conflicting emotions. On the one hand, she was aware that she now possessed evidence that could potentially expose Hart as a manipulative predator and possibly even a murderer. On the other hand, however, was the irresistible magnetic pull of her undeniable attraction to him. And in that moment, when he had held her wrist and gazed intently at her, she'd felt the attraction may be reciprocated. She had long ago taught herself to be governed by reason rather than emotion, but Hart's effect on her was so strong that she felt her resolve crumbling. She was torn in two between her sense of duty and justice and the dark allure of the professor.

Her phone buzzed, jolting her from her thoughts.

Lucas: Meet me in my office at 3 pm tomorrow. There's something important I need to discuss with you regarding your thesis.

Sophia sighed and shook her head at the imperative nature of the text. Hart was so full of his own importance that it wouldn't occur to him to check if she was free before arranging a meeting. But then, he had such a commanding presence that he would rarely be challenged. She certainly had no intention of disobeying him, as much as she would've liked to. He had a way of getting people to do his bidding without them even realizing it.

She was about to compose a reply when her heart skipped a beat. *Has he discovered the missing notebook? Is that what this text is really about?* By agreeing to meet him, she could be putting herself in danger once again. She momentarily considered telling Hart that she couldn't make it but reasoned that if he were already suspicious, her avoidance of him would only heighten those suspicions. She was trapped, and it was a trap that she had willingly walked into.

She texted him back.

Sophia: OK, I'll be there.

She threw her phone down in front of her alongside the notebook, but not before turning it off so that he couldn't contact her further. Just what was it about this man that made her abandon all sense of reason? Sophia didn't know the answer, but what she did know was that Lucas Hart had a hold over her so strong that even the knowledge that he may be a harmful predator couldn't and wouldn't keep her away from him. Like it or not, he had pulled her into his web, and she was stuck fast.

At precisely three o'clock the following afternoon, Sophia stood outside Hart's office, her hand trembling slightly as she knocked on the door. "Come in," he called, his voice as calm and composed as always. She entered the room, and their eyes met, causing the increasingly familiar thrill of excitement to jolt through her. Hart was seated behind his desk, the scene of yesterday's crime. Determined not to give him the upper hand, Sophia refused to break eye contact as he greeted her. "Sophia, I'm so glad you came. Please take a seat." His voice was so warm and friendly that she almost forgot what she suspected him of. Almost.

Sophia sat down and tried to take a few surreptitious breaths to steady herself, although fear wasn't the dominant driver of her anxiety. She quickly composed herself, and her voice was steady when she spoke. "You said you wanted to discuss my thesis, Lucas?"

Hart leaned back in his chair in that playful manner of his, his eyes not once leaving her face. "Indeed I did. I've been thinking about your research on manipulation, and yesterday, I had a 'Eureka!' moment. Have you ever considered exploring some of the darker aspects?"

Sophia's eyes narrowed. "What do you mean by 'the darker aspects'?" she asked.

Hart gave her one of his enigmatic smiles, and Sophia felt as though the air had left the room. "Oh, I think you know." His voice was so low it was almost a caress, and Sophia shivered involuntarily. Lucas continued. "The true power of manipulation lies in domination, the ability to control. Have you ever thought about what it would be like to wield that kind of power, Sophia? So you could write about it from first-hand experience?"

Sophia's mind raced ahead as she tried to ascertain where the conversation was going. She suspected that Hart was testing her, trying to push her boundaries. "I'd be lying if I said I'd never thought about it," she answered slowly. "After all, it would be a truly unique direction for my research and give me some great material for my thesis. But it's a dangerous path to take. I'm not sure I'm ready."

Hart's eyes gleamed as though she'd given him the answer he sought. "Oh, you're not wrong," he breathed, "it's most definitely dangerous. But it's also exhilarating. Mastering the ability to bend others to your will, making them do your bidding—it's intoxicating. There's no doubt in my mind that you're ready."

Sophia felt the last of her willpower slipping away and desperately attempted to cling on to it. "I understand what you're saying, and yes, I agree. But as well as all those things, it's also terrifying. The potential for harm is immense."

Hart leaned toward her, his hypnotic eyes trained on her face. "My point exactly. Fear is a powerful tool, Sophia, but it can also be a barrier. Don't let it come between you and complete comprehension of manipulative power. I know you can do this. I've never been so certain of anything in my life. You're a brilliant student, Sophia, and you have what it takes. This is the chance for you to make a name for yourself in the academic world, and it would be thoroughly deserved. You must conquer your fears to avoid letting the opportunity pass you by."

It took all Sophia's restraint not to let out an audible moan. Sitting at his desk in the weak afternoon sunlight, Lucas had an almost ethereal beauty, and he was saying exactly what she wanted to hear. It was a heady and irresistible combination. She was astute enough to know that, on some level, she was somehow becoming the victim of his manipulation. But she didn't care. At that moment, nothing was more important to her than her attraction to him and the darkness he represented.

"I'll try," she whispered, caught in the moment.

Hart's smile widened. "Excellent," he said. "I knew you'd make the right decision. I have such high hopes for you, and under my guidance, there's no way you can fail. Let's revisit your work so far and see how it can help us move forward."

Fortunately for Sophia, Hart seemed not to notice her lack of enthusiasm or concentration as they reviewed her progress on her thesis. She was reeling, not just from what he'd suggested she do but more from her willingness to comply. By the time she left his office, her mind and body were completely in conflict with one another. She couldn't fool herself any longer that she wasn't physically, mentally, and emotionally falling head over heels for him. But she also knew what he was capable of and had the evidence to prove it. *What does that say about me? Am I complicit in his crimes now?* The more time she spent in his company, the more attracted to him she became. Why was she letting that outweigh her growing fear of him? *Am I so entangled in his web that I've willingly cut off all forms of escape?*

All these questions and more whirled around in her mind as she walked home from the campus. She soon, however, became distracted by another more immediate sensation. She had the strong feeling that she was being watched. She quickened her pace and stole a nervous glance behind her, relieved when no one was there. But her relief was short-lived when a figure stepped out of the shadows in front of her, completely blocking her path.

The stranger's build indicated a female, but it was difficult to tell as she was wearing a baseball cap pulled low and a scarf pulled high around her neck. She seemed, if anything, even more anxious than Sophia. "You're Sophia Reed, right?" she asked, her voice low and urgent.

"Yes, that's right," replied Sophia. "But who are you, and how do you know who I am? And why are you following me?"

As the stranger stepped closer, Sophia could see the part of her face that wasn't obscured by clothing and realized that she wasn't much older than herself—in her mid-to-late twenties at most.

The stranger stepped closer, turning her face away from Sophia's. "It doesn't matter who I am," she hissed. "I'm just warning you to stay away from Lucas Hart. He's dangerous. I know you think he's helping you with your research, but his motives are much darker."

Sophia's blood ran cold. "How on earth do you know about my research?" she asked.

"It doesn't matter," the stranger repeated, looking around nervously. "Just stay away from Hart. He's not who he seems. He's been manipulating students for years and using them to experiment with to further his career and indulge his desires. Emily Warren could vouch for that if she were still alive. Please don't kid yourself into thinking that he thinks you're special; you're one of many. You're just his latest obsession."

Sophia felt her blood pressure rising. "How do you know all this?" she asked.

The stranger's eyes inexplicably filled with tears. "I can't tell you that," she said, "but believe me when I tell you I know what he's capable of. You need to get away from him before it's too late."

Sophia could sense the stranger's waves of fear. "What do you mean 'before it's too late'?" she whispered.

The female glanced around again before replying. "Hart's experiments... they're not purely academic. There's a personal aspect to them, too. He's willing to do whatever it takes to prove his theories, and he doesn't care how many ethical and legal boundaries he crosses. It's not just a professional thing; it's for pleasure, too. I don't think... Emily's death... it wasn't as cut and dried as it seems."

"Are you saying he killed her?" Sophia felt the chill wash over her as she said the words.

"It's not as simple as that." The stranger's voice was breaking up. "There would have been manipulation involved and people pushed to breaking point. And then an innocent victim was murdered. She was just collateral damage."

Sophia's mind reeled from the stranger's revelations. *How much truth is there in these allegations?* There was undoubtedly some correlation with what she had already suspected. But could the man she was falling for so deeply be so consumed with darkness that he would kill to prove a point? "Why are you telling me this?" she finally asked the stranger.

"Because I don't want you to become his next victim. Please be careful, Sophia. Hart's dangerous, and he won't hesitate to hurt you like he hurt the others."

The others? thought Sophia. *How many more are there?* But the stranger hadn't finished.

"Please listen to me, Sophia," she was saying. "I think you know this already. And you know what you need to do to stop him. Find proof and expose him. But you need to be careful; he's always watching."

This last sentence seemed too much for the stranger, and with a strangled sob, she took off at speed into the shadows, leaving Sophia with a plethora of unanswered questions. She was scared, confused, and had no idea what to do or whom to trust. The stranger's testimony seemed to fit with Sophia's own theories about Hart. *But if she knows so much, why hasn't she gone to the police? How long has she been following me? How does she know so much about me? What's her motive? Jealousy?* Sophia could easily see how Hart could become the victim of an obsessed student, but she also knew that his record wasn't as squeaky clean as he would have others believe. She suspected him of involvement in Emily Warren's murder, but did she really think he was capable of such a callous act? The only thing that she knew for sure was that someone was playing a dangerous game, and—for some reason—she was caught right in the middle. She needed to trust her instincts and discover the truth, no matter the cost.

The only barrier to her goal was her obsession with the man at the very heart of the deception, who now had so much control over her that it terrified her.

Sophia fell into a troubled sleep that night with the stranger's words racing around in her head. But one phrase repeatedly returned to her: "He's always watching." *What does that mean? Is he watching me now?*

5

The Spiral

Peaceful sleep eluded Sophia that night and the nights that followed, reawakening a long-dormant dread in her mind and body. Following her breakup with Jamie, insomnia had been a barrier to her recovery, and she had sworn she would never put herself through anything like that again. And yet here she was, tossing and turning, feeling like she was losing control of everything. When she did eventually manage to snatch some sleep, her dreams were littered with images of Emily Warren's lifeless body and Lucas Hart's icy blue eyes. She would wake up in a cold sweat with her heart racing, unable in the dim light of her bedroom to distinguish what was real and what existed only in the dark recesses of her mind. She knew from experience that her descent into the darkness would be swift and relentless unless she reclaimed her nights and restored a healthy sleep pattern. But right now, she was incapable of doing so.

It didn't take long for the effects of her insomnia to seep into the daytime, too. In the days that followed her impromptu meeting with the stranger, she started to move through her routines like a robot; her mind was fogged with lack of sleep, fear and desire. It wasn't long before her friends and tutors began to notice the change in her, but she became adept at brushing off their concerns with false smiles and reassurances, as she had in the early days after she and Jamie separated. She repeated the phrase, "I'm fine, just stressed about my thesis," like a mantra until she almost started believing it herself. Eventually, people stopped asking.

In truth, Sophia was far from fine. Her mental health was unraveling at an alarming rate. However, she refused to give up on her investigation, determined to somehow uncover the facts. Unfortunately, the deeper she delved into her quest, the more the lines between reality and imagination seemed to blur. She began to have visions—catching sight of fleeting shadows out of the corner of her eye that disappeared when she whipped her head around to confront them. She even heard disembodied voices whispering in her ear but could never decipher what they were saying. It was as if her nightmares refused to stay in the darkness where they belonged and were determined to haunt her days as well.

One afternoon, as she walked across the campus following yet another lecture where she had struggled to stay awake, she saw a familiar figure leaning up against a wall. With growing horror, Sophia realized it was Emily Warren, staring directly at her with hollow, accusatory eyes. Sophia blinked once, and Emily vanished, replaced by a group of students who were chatting animatedly, none of them looking as though they had just seen the ghost of a murder victim. Sophia shook her head in a futile attempt to clear the fog in her brain. She just needed to stay focused—she was so close to finding the proof she needed to either expose Hart as a dangerous predator or prove his innocence.

Despite the mounting evidence against him, Sophia was becoming increasingly fascinated by Hart and was starting to hope that her initial suspicions were unjust. She knew that she was potentially putting herself in danger, but her rising obsession with him was consuming her just as much as her investigation into whether he was involved in a brutal murder. Between lectures and their mentoring sessions, she was still spending a significant amount of time in his company. She was intoxicated by his presence and captivated by his intellect, even though all the information she was uncovering pointed to his guilt.

As well as conducting her personal investigation into Emily's murder and Professor Hart's background, Sophia was determined to continue with her thesis and research into the psychology of manipulation. Despite being exhausted almost to the point of physical sickness, she visited the university library daily to research Dark Triad Influence, dark charisma, and real-life cases where perpetrators displaying these traits had committed heinous crimes. Hart himself had written many of the articles she read, and many others cited his work. He had undoubtedly proved himself to be the leading scientist in the field, and no one else came close. *What drove him to dedicate his life to such dark topics?* It took everything Sophia had to remain focused on her work, but she was determined to continue despite feeling herself slipping further down into the black hole of darkness.

The police investigation into Emily's murder hadn't uncovered any new evidence for a while, causing Sophia's progress to plateau as there was less and less for her to go on. And every time she tried to dig into Professor Hart's past, she swore that even less information was available than the last time she had checked. It was almost as though someone was systemically erasing his personal history from the archives, although she knew that couldn't be correct. *Really? Is he somehow spying on me now, here in the library, waiting for me to slip up and make a mistake?* The thought caused a thrill of apprehension to travel up her spine, but the idea of being watched by Hart excited her more than she cared to admit.

Sophia also continued to attend her mentoring sessions with him, determined that her thesis shouldn't suffer for their actions any more than it had to. One evening, after a particularly intense session in his office, Hart placed his hand gently on her arm as she was about to walk out the door. "Sophia," he began, his voice soft and intimate. "Forgive me if I'm speaking out of turn, but you've been working so hard. You deserve a break; take some time to clear your mind."

Sophia's eyes widened as she looked up at him, and her heartbeat accelerated. "I can't, Lucas," she said. "Time's running out, and there's too much at stake. My thesis has to take priority right now."

Hart smiled gently at her. "You're too hard on yourself, Sophia. Taking care of yourself should come first. You're more important than any thesis." He reached out and gently brushed a stray strand of hair from her face in an unmistakably intimate gesture, taking Sophia's breath away.

She shivered, unable to ignore his proximity. He was so close that she could feel the warmth radiating from his body and smell the faint scent of his expensive cologne. Her mind was screaming at her to pull away, trying to remind her of the danger he represented. But her body wouldn't let her, her desire for him overpowering every sense of reason.

Then, their eyes locked, and Sophia's world tilted on its axis. Hart's hand moved to her cheek, lingering there before he traced a gentle line along her jaw with his thumb. Sophia's breath hitched, and her eyes closed. She automatically leaned into him, involuntarily parting her lips to receive his kiss.

But just as his lips brushed hers, his cell phone, which had been sitting silently on his desk throughout their meeting, rang loudly.

Returning to Earth with a bump, Sophia stepped away from him, not knowing whether the color flooding her cheeks was from desire or shame. "I… I should go," she stammered as he glanced at his now silent phone, lying unanswered on the desk.

Hart gazed at her for a moment. His face wore its usual mask of unreadability, but Sophia was sure she detected a flicker of darkness in his eyes.

"Of course, if that's what you want. Take care, Sophia." His tone was light and friendly but held none of the intimacy he had shown her just moments before. *Did I imagine it?*

Sophia felt a sob rise in her throat as she turned and hurried out the door. She was overcome with emotions, all of which felt like they were battling to escape her body. There was no doubt that she wanted Hart, physically, emotionally, and in every other way possible. And a moment ago, it had looked like he wanted her, too. But she couldn't ignore her suspicions, her gut feeling that he was a very dangerous man, backed by the evidence she was slowly uncovering.

That night, as she lay in bed, it was as if her mind was punishing her for her body's misdemeanors by replaying the close encounter with Lucas over and over. Hot shame washed over her as she realized what she had almost done with a man she suspected of murder. She knew if Lucas had kissed her, she wouldn't have stopped him. She groaned softly, thinking of how it would have felt had he pulled her close, so she melted into him. It was as though her body and mind had declared war on one another, and her body was winning, having all but erased her mind's defenses. She had no idea how to recover from this. *If suspecting him of being a killer isn't enough to stop me falling for him, then I don't know what is!*

For once, Sophia was almost grateful not to fall asleep as she knew her dreams would be full of her and Lucas and what might have been. She desperately tried to think how she could extricate herself from his clutches, but she couldn't see a way that meant he could still help her with her thesis. At least, that was what she told herself. In truth, she wanted to be more involved with him, not less, and the realization terrified her.

Following another torturous sleepless night, Sophia got up the following day with a strengthened resolve. Her emotions might have been winning the battle when it came to Lucas Hart, but she could reinforce her mind's defenses by finding some concrete evidence she could take to the police, directly linking Hart to murder. Forgoing the university library for once, she headed instead to the Harefield public library, where she spent hours searching through archived records and files.

Leaving no stone unturned, she fact-checked every tiny detail she found on Hart, hoping to uncover the link she so desperately needed. It was painstaking work that took its toll on her already sleep-deprived brain. Only briefly leaving the reference section once to grab some lunch, she trawled through every acknowledgment to Hart she could find, cross-referencing it with what she already knew.

Hours later, the words were swimming in front of her eyes. She sighed wearily and decided to give it one more hour before calling it a day. The words "needle" and "haystack" were at the forefront of her mind. She had decided to check police reports for any historical murders with circumstances similar to Emily's that somehow had a link to Hart, no matter how tenuous. She was struggling to focus, barely taking in what she was reading. But then she found something that made her blood run cold, and she sat up straight in her chair, suddenly alert.

It was a police report from several years ago. A girl in her early twenties had been murdered in gruesome circumstances, just like Emily. The girl had no connection to Hart—she had just qualified as a lawyer at another university. The case had gone cold and never been resolved, as Emily's was in danger of doing, as there were no witnesses and the police had retrieved very little evidence from the scene. Apart from the similar circumstances, nothing in particular linked the two cases. But it was a grainy photo attached to the report that grabbed Sophia's attention and made her hurry over to one of the library's ancient computers and fire up the internet.

Ten minutes later, Sophia stood at the library's printer, gathering all the evidence she needed to link Hart to that murder and also, potentially, to the murder of Emily Warren. The picture that was the catalyst for Sophia's discovery was of the grieving family of the first victim, who was named Laura, looking distraught in one of the first statements they gave to the press:

Laura was a clever and kind girl with her whole life ahead of her. She had never harmed a soul and did nothing to deserve what happened to her. She was very much loved by all who knew her, especially her parents, brothers and sister.

Laura's parents and her brothers were looking at the ground in the photo, their heads heavy with the weight of their grief. But her sister looked more terrified than anything else and was gazing off wildly into the distance. And it was the terrified gaze that ignited a spark of recognition in Sophia.

Her mind raced to piece together the puzzle, all thoughts of fatigue forgotten. Laura was obviously named in the report, so it wasn't difficult to find the names of her family members, including her sister, and run a background check on their social media accounts. Laura had been a law student at a different university, but her sister, Julie, studied psychology at Harefield. Julie went on to specialize in Dark Triad Influence and dark charisma under the mentorship of Professor Lucas Hart. And she was the stranger who had previously accosted Sophia in the street.

The puzzle wasn't yet complete, but Sophia now had a much clearer view of the big picture. Hart had been manipulating his students for years, using them as subjects in his twisted experiments. And the outcome seemed to be murder. Feeling nauseous, Sophia considered her next move. This was the proof she'd been looking for, so she should really take it straight to the police. *What's stopping me?* Gathering the papers into her backpack, she prepared to leave the library. But as she reached the door, she felt a presence behind her and spun around to confront them. No one was there, just the elderly librarian behind the desk, absorbed in her work. Sophia's mind was playing tricks on her again.

She realized she was shaking and took a deep breath to calm herself. This was the time to be strong; she couldn't afford to buckle under the weight of her discovery. She knew she needed to trust her instincts and take her evidence to the police. But she couldn't.

Instead, she walked home slowly, clutching her backpack tightly to her chest as though it was the only thing holding her together. With every step she took, she felt as though Hart was behind her, following, watching, and waiting. She was running out of time to decide where her loyalties lay, as withholding evidence made her as guilty as Hart. But she couldn't bring herself to do it, even in light of this latest discovery. She couldn't end the career and the freedom of the man who had become her obsession. He still had so much more to teach her.

6

Confrontations

Sophia arrived at Hart's office the following day as planned for their mentoring meeting, her mind racing with conflicting thoughts and feelings. She clenched her backpack tightly, knowing its contents were a ticking time bomb of evidence that could destroy her mentor's reputation. She had spent the entire night grappling with the realization that someone she respected and had deep feelings for could be capable of murder. The moral and legal dilemma weighed heavily on her, leaving her feeling drained and exhausted. As she stood in front of Hart's office door, her hand poised to knock, she felt like a puppet, controlled by the strings of her emotions. She knew she had to confront him, but the thought made her stomach churn. She took a deep breath and knocked.

"Come in," Hart called from inside.

Sophia entered, her eyes scanning the setting of Hart's office. Everything was in order—the familiar bookshelves lining the walls, the neatly organized desk, and the comfortable armchair where she usually sat. But today, the atmosphere was different. The air felt thicker than usual with tension, and the warmth she normally felt in his presence was gone.

"Good morning, Sophia," Hart greeted her, his voice giving nothing away.

Sophia's smile was strained as she tried to suppress the knot of fear in her stomach. She closed the door behind her, attempting to control the trembling in her hands. She hoped Lucas wouldn't pick up on her nerves. "Lucas, I need to talk to you before we start," she said, her voice wavering.

Hart's smile faded, replaced by the predictable mask of inscrutability. "Okay," he said slowly. "What's on your mind?"

Sophia approached his desk and placed her backpack on it. She unzipped it and retrieved the police report with shaking hands. She took a deep breath and began to explain, her voice shaking with nerves. "I found this yesterday. It's a police report from several years ago about a girl named Laura who died in suspicious circumstances. Her sister, Julie, is a former student of yours."

Hart's confusion was evident on his face. Sophia continued, hoping against all hope that he would provide some sort of explanation to put her mind at ease. "The details of the murder are remarkably similar to the Emily Warren case."

Hart remained silent, his face a stony mask. He reached out his hand, wordlessly requesting the report Sophia still clutched tightly.

Her hands still shook as she passed it to him, her eyes following his every move. *Is he attempting to hide his feelings? Or is he just a master of deception?*

After scanning through the pages, he finally spoke up. "And what do you make of this?"

Sophia was caught off guard. She had expected a fierce denial, not to be immediately questioned herself. Without stopping to think, she blurted out the accusation that had lived in her mind for weeks. "I think it means you've been manipulating your students and using them for your experiments, the end results of which are fatal.."

Hart's piercing gaze bore into her and gave away nothing of what he was thinking or feeling.

Is he sad? Disappointed? Or something much darker?

"Listen, I don't know where you got this information from, but it's not what you think."

As Sophia processed his dismissive response, all the effects of her insomnia and repressed emotions came flooding to the surface. She braced herself, knowing that a confrontation was imminent. "It's exactly what I think!" The words burst free from her mouth as tears streamed down her face. Her clear, green eyes reflected the pain and anger she had been holding back for so long.

Hart calmly held her gaze. "Sophia, you're under a great deal of stress with your thesis, and you're letting your imagination run wild. Yes, Julie was a student of mine, and she was struggling with her mental health. Her sister was heading down a dark path, and the whole family felt the strain. After graduating from law school, Laura went off the rails with alcohol, drugs, and such. She soon fell in with an extremely bad crowd. She and Julie were so close it was inevitable that Julie would be affected. And yes, Julie was part of my research back then, but I was trying to help her. I never did anything to harm her."

His words cut through Sophia's mind like a knife, fueling her inner conflict rather than soothing it. As much as she respected and desired him, she still felt he was holding back. "You're right; I am under a lot of stress," she said, trying to compose herself, "but that doesn't change the fact that this report is evidence that you may be connected to a murder with a similar modus operandi to Emily's—a case in which you've shown an unhealthy interest."

Hart's expression didn't falter, and Sophia felt her confidence waning.

"Do you know what happened to Laura?" she whispered.

Hart nodded, and Sophia's stomach flipped.

"Laura was a troubled young woman," explained Hart, his voice gentle but firm. "Unfortunately, her demise was inevitable, whether by her own hand or that of others. There was a complication, as her boyfriend was the son of a prominent senator who didn't want his name involved. So much of the investigation was kept under wraps, eventually disappearing altogether. I know this because Julie told me about it herself. In the end, Laura made her own choices, and I'm sure Emily Warren did the same."

"Why didn't you help her?" Sophia cried, all attempts at staying in control cast to the wind. "If Julie told you that Laura was mixed up with the wrong crowd and was in danger, why didn't you intervene?"

"I couldn't." Hart's façade cracked momentarily, and his eyes betrayed the tiniest hint of guilt.

Or is that wishful thinking?

"Laura was neither my student nor my patient. I knew of the senator's son's involvement and had my professional reputation to protect. I also couldn't afford to lose another job. No matter how much I wanted to, it was a line I couldn't cross."

Sophia's resolve wavered as she listened to Hart's words. She couldn't deny that his explanation made sense, but she also couldn't ignore the doubts and fears that plagued her. Lucas's calm demeanor and logical reasoning only added to her confusion. His explanation certainly sounded plausible. She had always prided herself on her keen academic mind, but now she wondered if her judgment was emotionally driven. She was stressed and sleep-deprived. *Perhaps fear and paranoia are getting the better of me?* "But the similarities between the two murders..."

"Are coincidences," Hart interrupted. He placed the report on his desk, walked around the front to where Sophia stood, and took both of her hands in his.

She couldn't help but feel a sense of comfort and reassurance, but at the same time, she felt a twinge of guilt for betraying her own beliefs and suspicions. She knew deep down that she should trust her instincts but couldn't stop the doubt from creeping in. Her usually tidy mind was now a jumbled mess, torn between loyalty and desire for her mentor and her gut instinct about his guilt. She had been so sure of her theory, but now she was questioning everything. *Am I just grasping at straws?*

"Look, Sophia, you're a brilliant student with one of the best academic minds I've ever encountered. But right now, you're listening to your emotions and ignoring reason. Come on, you're better than this."

As Hart urged her to think rationally, Sophia's thoughts tumbled around her mind, a jumble of confusion and doubt. She had been so sure, but now, with Lucas standing in front of her, being so calm and reasonable, holding her hands, guiding her... She sighed, trying to blow away the doubts and fears, but they lingered like a dark cloud. "I just don't know what to believe anymore," she finally admitted, the self-doubt evident in her voice. She couldn't believe she was questioning her core beliefs, but she also couldn't deny how much Hart's words and presence impacted her. Looking into his eyes, she couldn't help but wonder if he was manipulating her, playing on her emotions to sway her, as part of his twisted agenda. But their intense chemistry made him difficult to resist. Her inner turmoil intensified as she stood there, torn. She knew she had to make a choice, but the thought of betraying him was almost more than her conscience could bear. She was stuck at a moral intersection, unsure which path was the right one.

Sophia's heart raced as Lucas released her hands and gently cupped her face instead. She knew she should push him away, but his touch was so gentle, so comforting. Her mind swayed between fearing him and trusting him. Self-belief hadn't been a problem for her recently. Until now.

"Just believe in yourself, Sophia," Hart said softly as though reading her mind while still gazing into her eyes. "Trust your instincts. You know I would never do anything to harm any of my students intentionally. And I would certainly never hurt you."

Sophie's breath hitched as he touched her face, their eyes locked together with her heart pounding painfully in her chest. She desperately wanted to believe and trust him, but her doubts wouldn't let her. *What if I've got this wrong? What if he's guilty?* But then again, he was her professor and mentor; she couldn't envisage him ever harming his students. But that was precisely what the evidence suggested, taunting her and making her question everything she thought she knew. In a trembling voice, she whispered, "I'm scared, Lucas."

He pulled her into an embrace, his hands now on her waist, and murmured reassuringly into her ear. "I know you are, Sophia. But you needn't be. I'll take care of you."

As Sophia sank into his arms, the warmth from his body melted the icy cold fear in her heart. She had her suspicions about him when she entered his office, but her heart now overruled her head as he held her, and all she could think about was how much she wanted him. She couldn't ignore their chemistry, but it didn't stop the conflicting emotions from racing through her mind.

He pulled back from her slightly, still keeping his eyes locked on hers. "You're a strong woman, Sophia," he told her. "Much stronger than you realize. You're far too strong to let your fear control you. Let go of it and embrace your feelings."

But Sophia couldn't just let go of her fear. She had built impenetrable walls around her heart to protect herself from getting hurt again. She couldn't afford to let Hart break them down, especially now. He was charming and sophisticated, but the sense that he was hiding something was too strong to ignore.

And then he leaned toward her, his breath warm against her skin, his hand brushing her arm, leaving a trail of fire in its wake.

She couldn't resist the pull toward him, her body aflame with desire as his lips brushed against hers. At that moment, reality meant nothing compared to her overwhelming need for him. The taste of him was like a drug, intoxicating and addictive. She couldn't get enough of it, so she opened her mouth to deepen the kiss, reveling in the passion of his response. Every touch, every caress, sent waves of ecstasy throughout her body. She was consumed by him and by the way he made her feel. The depth of their connection drowned out every last remnant of fear and doubt. She pulled him closer, her fingers digging into his hair, lost in the moment. Their passion was a fierce storm that bound them together, blurring the lines between what was real and what wasn't. Nothing else existed in time but the two of them, their bodies pressed together, connected on a level beyond the physical.

When they finally pulled apart, both of them were breathless, their chests heaving. As he looked at her, his intense eyes smoldering with desire, Sophia felt like she was seeing him for the first time. He was complex and intriguing, but irresistible. She couldn't stay away if she tried.

"Sophia..." His voice was a husky whisper, sending shock waves through her body.

Tears welled in her eyes as her emotions overflowed. But then she made an unwelcome return to reality as the implications of what had just happened between her and her professor hit her with full force. "I'm sorry," she stammered, her voice thick with embarrassment. "I don't know who I am anymore."

Sophia felt like a lost lamb as Hart gently smoothed her hair back from her face. His touch was like a feather, soft and tender, yet it still made her shiver with pleasure. "I can help you, Sophia," he said softly, his words intensifying the electricity flowing between them. "You're discovering your authentic self for the first time. It's who you're meant to be. Embrace it." And then he kissed her again, igniting the fire within her that threatened to rage out of control.

Sophia's heart pounded as she released her inhibitions and allowed her desires to take command. Her heart beat wildly as she succumbed to his charms, allowing him to take their passion to new heights. She was powerless to resist him; such was the strength of their attraction. In that moment, she needed him like she needed oxygen to breathe—there could be no compromise. While under the spell of his kisses, she believed in his innocence completely, and no amount of evidence in the world could persuade her otherwise. He had explained, and she fully accepted his explanation. She didn't know why she had ever doubted him; she trusted him wholeheartedly. All her doubts and fears melted away in the heat of his embrace.

But as they pulled apart and gazed into each other's eyes again, Sophia felt the stirrings of doubt once more. *Is this all part of his game?* She had gone to his office intending to expose him, but now she didn't see how she could. *Suppose he tells the authorities that I tried to seduce him, and he resisted my advances? They'll just think I'm a scorned student out looking for revenge. Is this part of his trap?* She felt the sudden need to distance herself before she was entirely con-sumed by him. She still wanted him, but she knew better than to let her emotions rule her head. There was more to discover about Lucas Hart, of that she was sure, and she was determined to un-ravel the hitherto hidden complexities of his character. But for now, she needed to focus on keeping some distance and not suc-cumbing to his intoxicating presence. She couldn't let herself get further pulled into his web, no matter how tempted she was.

7

The Descent

When Sophia finally left Hart's office, she felt as though her world was unraveling. She walked home thinking of their passionate encounter, but Hart's apparent indifference to the evidence she had uncovered also occupied her mind. If sleep had been difficult for her before, it was now impossible. The nights that followed bled into days and the days into nights. Her once orderly life had disintegrated into a chaotic mess involving insomnia, frantic research, and an obsession with Hart that grew more and more unhealthy by the day. Fantasy and reality became blurred in her mind, the lines of demarcation lost in a haze of fear, doubt, and desire. After that night, she and Hart had agreed to postpone their next meeting for a week—ostensibly so that Sophia could conduct some research into Machiavellianism, but in reality, it was to give them both some time to process what had happened, and the accusations Sophia had unwittingly blurted out.

Although she desperately wanted to concentrate on her thesis, Sophia was plagued by visions of Lucas Hart wherever she went. If, with a little help from Ambien, she was able to catch a few moments of sleep, she saw him in her dreams. He existed in the shadows of her apartment and the faces of strangers she passed in the street. It seemed to Sophia that there was no escape from him and that he was holding her against her will in a magnetic force field that she could feel but not see. His gravitational pull was too strong for her to resist despite her still being unsure if the evidence she found in the library connected him to at least one gruesome murder. The conflict between her passionate desire for him and her suspicions that he might be capable of killing for fun was escalating to the point that it was driving her to the brink of a breakdown.

She tried her hardest to block thoughts of him from her mind by throwing herself headlong into her research.

People displaying high traits of Machiavellianism tend to view others as tools they can use to achieve their own goals. The link between Machiavellianism and manipulation lies in the Machiavellian's tendency to use deceptive strategies to achieve their objectives, often at the expense of others.

The words on the textbook page triggered a red flag in Sophia's mind. Wasn't that precisely what she was accusing Hart of doing? Of using his students for his twisted research into how far one human being can manipulate another? To see if he could push someone to commit murder against their will, simply for the thrill of being the first scientist to have done so?

It was a massive accusation, and the more it played on Sophia's mind, the more ridiculous it sounded. Sure, Hart had a superior understanding of manipulation tactics and how to execute them unnoticed, but he was a respected authority figure who had gained the trust of many, not to mention that he was highly attractive and persuasive, so people tended to trust him naturally. He did not need to manipulate them into doing so. Also, what about the passion between them the last time they'd met? If he had staged that, it would mean he was remorseless and more than willing to engage in unethical and harmful behaviors to achieve his goals. He had been so gentle and patient with her, and she had felt the heat of his desire as much as her own. There was simply no way it could have been a strategic move to stop her from blowing his cover. The sexual tension had been building between them for too long.

Sophia was contemplating this with the textbook open in front of her when her phone buzzed with a text from Lucas.

Lucas: Please come to my office, Sophia. I need to talk to you.

Sophia's heart sank. They had both agreed she needed some distance from him for a while to at least pretend to concentrate on her studies. She picked up her phone to reply, intending to remind him of this. But the thought of his intoxicating presence was too much for her to resist. She imagined being in his arms again with his lips locked on hers, both of them surrendering to the flames of passion. She knew the sensible thing to do would be to stay away, but she didn't have the strength to pull against his magnetism. Besides, seeing him might be precisely what she needed to clear her mind—to convince herself she was being ridiculous and there was no way he was capable of what she suspected.

She walked through the deserted campus, the buildings casting eerie shadows in the twilight. This did nothing to calm her anxious mind; her nerves were like a tightly coiled spring. As she approached his office, she almost talked herself out of meeting him. But the flash of resolve failed her, and she once again found herself in the familiar position of knocking on his door.

"Come in," he called.

She entered the room to find him seated at his desk, where so much had happened between them. She glanced at his face in case it held any clues as to why he had requested to see her, but his expression gave nothing away, and neither did his voice when he invited her to take a seat.

She sat on the edge of the comfy armchair, her heart racing too fast for her to settle. "Lucas, I thought we agreed this wasn't a good idea for a while."

Hart, by contrast, seemed totally at ease. "I know what we said, Sophia, but some things have come to my attention, and I'm worried about you."

Sophia looked confused. "What do you mean?" she asked.

"Some of your tutors have expressed their concern," he replied, "They're saying that you haven't been yourself, and they're afraid you're pushing yourself too hard. Knowing you as I do, I have to say I agree. They think it's all down to your thesis, but I know how consumed you've been with your little obsession about these murders, not to mention what happened between us the other night."

He smiled gently at her, and Sophia had the grace to blush. "You're right, I'm struggling to think straight," she admitted. "I don't know what's happening to me."

"It's just stress and exhaustion, Sophia. You need to stop worrying about what doesn't concern you, like these murders, and focus on what's important, like your thesis."

Sophia's eyes stung with unshed tears as she shook her head. "I can't just let it go," she said. "I need to know what happened to those girls. I think you know more than you're letting on, and I want to understand. But I need to know the truth."

"Sophia." His voice was as gentle as a tender caress. "You can't possibly think that of me after what happened between us. I know you feel our connection as strongly as I do. You've got to trust me."

Sophia felt the familiar blanket of confusion engulf her.

"You're such a clever woman; you already know the truth deep in your heart. Let me guide you and teach you to trust your instincts."

Sophia's mind buckled under the weight of her emotions once again. "But there's evidence, police reports, similarities…" she said weakly.

"All coincidences," Hart repeated firmly. "Come on, Sophia, you know better than this. You're seeing patterns that don't exist because you're so desperate to find them and prove yourself as a scientist. You're connecting them with me because you're ashamed of your feelings and trying to convince yourself I'm not worthy of them. It's all in your head, and you would see that, if only you'd let yourself step back and take a break."

"But you knew about Laura, and Julie was your student, and there was that notebook with Emily's initials…"

Hart frowned here, and Sophia realized she'd slipped up by revealing she was aware of the notebook. He remained silent, however, so she continued. "I want to believe you, but I'm not sure I can." Her voice was barely more than a whisper.

Hart's eyes narrowed. He got up, walked around his desk, and stood in front of Sophia. "Look, I want to help you, and I can. But you need to want to help yourself. And I need you to trust me."

Lucas's proximity reminded Sophia of all that had happened between them. She wanted nothing more than to reach out and melt into his arms again, with the heat from his body warming hers and the faint tang of his cologne tickling her nostrils. But her mind was screaming at her to see reason and consider the danger she could be in.

She heard him murmur, "Don't let your fear control you." He was so close to her that if he came another millimeter nearer, she wouldn't be able to prevent herself from wrapping her arms around his neck and pulling his lips onto hers…

"Have you ever considered the true nature of manipulation, Sophia, and the power it gives you over others?"

Sophia hadn't even realized she'd closed her eyes until they flew open. She stared at Hart, whose expression had changed and whose eyes were gleaming with darkness.

"What do you mean?" she asked him breathlessly.

Hart sat casually on the front of his desk and took one of her hands in his. "You know that manipulation is about control, about bending others to your will. But have you ever considered it a game that can be played for fun? Yes, it's dangerous, but it can be gratifying if you play it right."

Sophia's mind cast back to a time when he had asked her a similar question. At the time, she had wondered if he was testing her, pushing her to see how far she would go. *Is that what he's doing now?*

"But it's not just dangerous, Lucas," she answered slowly. "It's also immoral and unethical, not to mention probably illegal."

Hart flashed her one of his enigmatic smiles. "Yes, and that's what makes it so exhilarating," he replied. "It's about the ability to influence others, to guide their thoughts and actions... It's a power few people truly understand."

Sophia didn't want to believe what she was hearing. "But there are consequences," she argued. "What about the harm it could cause?"

Hart's pupils were so enlarged that his eyes appeared utterly black. "Sure, there are risks, Sophia. But those who master the art of manipulation can navigate those risks, turning them to their advantage."

Sophia wondered about the banging sound she could hear until she realized it was her heart beating against her ribcage. *Wait a minute, this sounds familiar.* Wasn't this what she was reading about the other night in the textbook on Machiavellianism? *I must be confused.* Lucas was talking about her thesis, not his own personal experience. He'd already pointed out how her stress and exhaustion were altering her perception, and this was the perfect example. She was trying to find drama where none existed. Her mind drifted for a moment, and she remembered constantly being called a drama queen by her ex-boyfriend Jamie shortly before she caught him cheating. And here she was, doing it again, in real danger of damaging both her professional and personal relationship with Lucas Hart. Realizing that she was mistaken about Hart should have brought Sophia some comfort, but instead, she still felt as though she was teetering on the edge of a precipice.

In the days that followed, Sophia heeded Hart's advice and stopped investigating the murders, instead focusing solely on her thesis. She continued her mentoring meetings with Lucas, although not as frequently as before. She had reached a point in her thesis where she needed to find some case studies to dissect, real-world examples of manipulative strategies used for criminal activity, like the one Lucas had used in his first lecture of the semester. Sophia's thesis was focused on manipulation tactics in interpersonal relationships than corporate crimes, so she looked for examples where individuals exhibiting dark charisma traits had used their charm to win over their partners, only to later manipulate and control them. Her mind flashed sadly back to Jamie, who had initially overwhelmed her with love and affection, only to devalue and discard her when she had given him her heart. Feeling grateful the experience had made her a much stronger person, Sophia headed to the university library to look for what she needed.

She found many documented cases on the internet of people using manipulation tactics to control their partners and force them to engage in criminal activity. They were all very sad, but none of them had the level of intensity that Sophia wanted to discuss in her thesis. But then she found something that caught her interest. The names had been changed for legal reasons, but it was a story of a male student called Joe who had begun a relationship with a female student (referred to as Lexi as in the article) from another university. Lexi was initially drawn to Joe's charm and confidence. Over time, Joe started to subtly manipulate Lexi, isolating her from her friends and family and making her increasingly dependent on Joe for emotional support and validation.

Once Joe had established control, he convinced Lexi to engage in criminal activity for illegal gains, such as fraud and theft. Joe used a combination of flattery, guilt, and fear to manipulate Lexi, making her believe these actions were necessary for their future together. She had no choice but to comply. He would tell her things like, "If you really love me, you'll help me with this," or "We need this money to secure our future." Lexi sadly died later in suspicious circumstances, although no one had been charged with her murder. While the police were aware of Joe's manipulative influence over her, he had never been charged with anything and later disappeared without a trace.

Sophia decided this was exactly the type of case study she needed for her thesis and set about researching it further. It wasn't easy at first to find any more details without having their actual real names. After hours of painstaking research, Sophia had pieced together enough of a timeline to cross-reference it with other documented cases, but she had drawn a blank. Therefore, she decided to trek across town to the Harefield Community Library and continue her research there, where she struck gold.

The Harefield Library's computers had fewer security filters than the university's, and Sophia was soon able to link the details with recent real-life cases. What she discovered made her blood run cold. It wasn't the revelation that Lexi was actually Emily Warren, who brought on the panic attack so severely that the ancient librarian had to call for a paramedic. It was the fact that Joe was really Robert, the son of a local university dean and former psychology student under the mentorship of Professor Lucas Hart.

8

Web of Lies

After Sophia had convinced the kind paramedic that she was going to be okay, she returned to her apartment, where she sat staring blankly at the walls. She felt suffocated by her latest discovery and all it implied. Despite the vortex of fear and confusion that continued to swirl around her mind, she could see with terrifying precision that she could no longer ignore her suspicions about Hart. This was just one coincidence too many and, in her mind, was definitive proof that he had been involved in both Laura's and Emily's murders. What troubled her the most, however, was the fact that he had managed to pull the wool over her eyes for so long. She was such an honest person and prided herself on her ability to see deception in others. *But you did see it,* a small voice inside her head pointed out. *You just chose to ignore it because you didn't want it to be true.* Sophia sighed and let a wave of misery wash over her as she realized just how deeply she had been caught in Hart's web of lies.

As hard as she tried, Sophia couldn't stop thinking about how Hart had callously manipulated her feelings to hide his wrongdoings. She had fallen hard for his charisma and charm, and he had used that to his advantage as soon as he realized she was suspicious of his involvement in the murders. Knowing that their passion wasn't real broke Sophia's heart, but she was also aware of the other connotations—like having to finish her thesis without Hart's help. *I don't think I can do it.* Her mind reeled from the betrayal, and her heart was heavy with sadness. She felt herself slipping into an emotional void, a place that she had previously visited a long time before. The memory of how devastating that had been for her and her loved ones was enough to pull her back from the brink, albeit only slightly.

She knew that she needed a distraction to stop herself from dwelling on her pain. So she reluctantly began gathering together all the evidence she had found pertaining to Hart's involvement in both murders in preparation for taking it to the police. As she pieced together the fragments of her investigation, the magnitude of Hart's involvement became glaringly apparent to her. Julie was Laura's sister and Hart's student. Robert was Emily's boyfriend and Hart's student. *Does that imply it was Lucas himself who committed the murders? If so, why haven't the police investigated and arrested him?* Sophia had so many unanswered questions, and the more she studied her evidence, the more she was convinced that Laura, Julie, Robert, and Emily were all unfortunate players in a much larger game. *But what's my role in all this? Why did he pay me so much attention? Am I to be his next victim?*

Although she didn't want to, she couldn't help replaying her encounters with Hart repeatedly in her head, remembering everything he said and did. All the subtle hints and thinly veiled threats... *How could I have been so blind?* And then, of course, there was the seduction, and Sophia's cheeks flamed as she remembered how much she had wanted him and how little time it took for her to surrender to her desires. But Hart showed every trait of a master manipulator, so it was little wonder she had succumbed so easily. He had the charm and charisma of a narcissist, the strategic planning skills of a Machiavellian, and the intimidating personality of a psychopath. Precisely the same traits as the criminals he discussed in his lectures—the same ones she studied for her thesis. *How did I let this happen?*

But Hart had made it his mission to gain her respect and trust, using every weapon in his arsenal to do so. And she *had* trusted him, believing he was sincere, especially in his regard for her. But this last piece of evidence had finally opened her eyes to the truth. Hart had been manipulating her all along, using her to further his own twisted agenda, the full nature of which she was yet to discover. All she knew was that innocent people had already died while he pursued his goals. She was determined she would not be next.

The words started to swim before her eyes as she studied the evidence in front of her, and Sophia couldn't tell if the tears clouding her eyes were from sadness, fear, or exhaustion. Hart had already taken so much from her, making her doubt herself and isolating her from her family and friends. *Well, it all ends tonight.* It was going to take every bit of strength she possessed to present her evidence to the police, but she wasn't going to let her misery deter her from bringing him to justice. She would proactively mitigate his influence by rebuilding her broken support system, starting immediately by doing something long overdue. *I need to call my mom.*

Sophia's head was pounding with the start of a migraine, and her heart raced alarmingly as she dialed the number. *How can I explain what's been happening without worrying her?* Sophia herself was only just realizing how close to the danger she was dancing. Her mother was an astute lady with a honed sense when it came to her daughter's safety. She would know straight away there was something amiss. However, Sophia also thought that explaining the situation out loud might help her gain some clarity around what was happening. She chewed on her lip as she waited for the call to connect.

"Hello?"

"Hi, Mom." Sophia's voice was shaking with trepidation, but she still felt comforted when her mother answered the call.

"Sophia!" She could hear the relief in her mother's tone. "I've been so worried about you. Is everything okay?"

"No, Mom, everything is not okay." Sophia could barely choke back her sobs. "I need to talk to you about what's been happening here. It involves Professor Lucas Hart."

"Your mentor?" her mother sounded surprised. "What about him?"

Sophia took a deep breath and tried to explain everything the best she could. She told her mother about Emily Warren's murder, Hart's strange behavior, the notebook she had found in his desk drawer, being accosted by a stranger in the street, Laura's murder, and Hart's connections to both Laura's sister and Emily's boyfriend. She mentioned that she had been attracted to Lucas but played down their passionate encounter to spare her mother's embarrassment.

"Oh no, Sophia, you poor thing. You must be terrified. Lucas Hart is such an internationally respected figure; it's no wonder you doubted yourself. Come home now so I can keep you safe. Talk to the dean of the university. Tell him you're having problems with Hart and ask if you can finish working on your thesis with a new tutor. Remotely, from home. That's what Jamie did, and it worked brilliantly for him."

"Jamie?" Alarm bells immediately sounded in Sophia's mind. "What's he got to do with it? I haven't spoken to him in years, and I didn't think you had either."

There was silence on the other end of the phone, and Sophia wondered briefly if the signal had dropped out. Then, her mother spoke again.

"I didn't mention anything to you because I knew how upset you'd be. And rightly so. I hated him too for what he did to you. But he left town for a while, and when he came back, he was a changed man. He studied remotely for his graduate degree and is now an extremely successful businessman. You should see the fancy car he drives!"

There was a pause.

"He's been around here asking about you a lot. I wouldn't entertain him at first. I was far too upset with him for the state he left you in. But he seemed so remorseful. He really convinced me he was sorry for how he treated you and that he'd regretted it ever since. He's so charming. He's even been helping me on weekends, doing a few jobs around the yard."

Sophia couldn't believe what she was hearing. "How could you be taken in by him again?" she asked.

"Well, the same way you were taken in by Professor Hart, I guess," her mother retorted, and Sophia detected a defensive edge.

"Well, look where that got me," she snapped, and there was silence on the other end of the line. Sophia closed her eyes and massaged the bridge of her nose.

"Sorry, Mom, I've been under a lot of stress. It was just a shock to hear his name after all this time, especially from you. You said he's been asking about me a lot. What did you tell him?"

"It's fine, honey, I understand. That's why I didn't tell you sooner; I knew you'd be upset. He was asking about your graduate degree, and I told him all about your thesis and that you were being mentored by Professor Hart. Jamie seemed to know a lot about him. He said he had read some of his work."

"Jamie's heard of Professor Hart?" The alarm bells in Sophia's head reached a crescendo. "How come?"

"Well, I don't know exactly." Her mother was starting to sound a bit dubious. "He just told me he was a fan of Hart's work and had studied some of his teachings as part of his business degree. Apparently, he owes much of his professional success to Hart." Sophia's mum sniffed. "I wonder what he'll say when he discovers his idol's a murderer?"

"You mustn't breathe a word of this to anyone," Sophia hissed, panic escalating inside her. "Especially not Jamie."

"Well, okay," said her mother. "Although I don't see what harm it would do. You can tell him yourself when you get back here."

"I can't come straight away." Suddenly, returning to her childhood home seemed like jumping out of the frying pan into the fire.

"Why not?" asked her mother.

"Because I need to take the evidence I've collected to the local police for a start," explained Sophia, "and then I have to speak to the dean about studying remotely for my thesis."

"But you're in danger there." Her mother sounded concerned.

"I'll be fine for another few days, a week at the most. I'm not having any more mentoring sessions with Lucas Hart, and once the police are involved, I'm sure he'll be suspended pending an investigation. Try not to worry about me."

"As if." Sophia could hear her mother fighting back tears down the phone line, and it drove yet another dagger through her heart. "Okay, if you're sure. I just want to protect you and keep you safe. But you're a strong, intelligent woman, Sophia. I know you can look after yourself. Just promise you'll call me every day and come home as soon as you can."

"I promise," whispered Sophia, unable to suppress her tears any longer. She chatted with her mother about more trivial matters for a few minutes before they said their goodbyes and hung up.

The comfort that Sophia got from hearing her mother's voice was short-lived. As soon as they ended their call, Sophia realized that her next step would involve talking to the police—something she didn't relish in the slightest, especially knowing that she would have to disclose her steamy liaison with Hart. But something else was troubling her now and filling her stomach with unease. According to her mother, it now appeared that her ex-boyfriend also had a connection with Hart, although Sophia couldn't fathom what it might be. *Is Jamie also implicated in the murders?* She knew for sure, however, that it meant she needed to tread carefully. Jamie lived in the same town as her mother and visited her on weekends. There was no way she could risk putting her mother in any sort of danger.

She decided to sleep on it and take the evidence to the police in the morning, although "sleep" seemed like an impossible destination. However, after tossing, turning, and replaying everything in her mind all night, Sophia decided she had no choice but to uncover the depth of Jamie's involvement before she took the matter to the police for the sake of her mother's safety. There was no one else she could turn to—this was something she'd have to do entirely alone. Although recent events had rocked her confidence, Sophia was determined to single-handedly uncover the truth and expose Hart for what he truly was.

Over the next few days, Sophia devoted herself to uncovering Jamie's connection to Hart, but without much luck. She had previously blocked Jamie on all of her social media accounts, but she unblocked him now only to find that her mother was correct and that he was, in fact, a highly successful businessman. After completing his graduate degree, he seemed to have had an almost meteoric rise to fame in the business world. The internet was full of sycophantic praise for him, and she subjected herself to watching hours of footage of his motivational speeches from all around the globe. She tried not to let it open old wounds but was surprised at how quickly the feelings of intense hurt came flooding back.

Her first few social media sweeps were informative but did not help her decipher Jamie's connection to Hart. She knew she would have to utilize all her investigative skills and return to the local library. She decided to stop at a bakery along the way to pick up a cake for the librarian who had been so kind to her on her last disastrous visit. Feeling more relaxed now that she was doing something positive, Sophia tossed her phone into her bag and headed out her apartment door. Just as she closed the door behind her, her phone rang.

Sophia cursed softly under her breath but dared not ignore the call in case it was her mother. *She'll only worry if I don't answer.* Rifling through her bag, she retrieved her cell phone just as the call dropped, only for it to start ringing again almost immediately. Seeing that it was an anonymous caller, Sophia nearly didn't answer it, but then she changed her mind. *It might be something important.*

"Hello?" she said when the call connected.

The caller hung up straight away.

Shrugging her shoulders and assuming it was the wrong number, Sophia tossed the phone back in her bag and walked down the stairs to the exit of her apartment block. Just as she reached the bottom, her phone rang again. Sighing with exasperation, she pulled it from her bag and answered it.

"Hello?" she repeated.

Again, the caller hung up immediately.

Sophia stuffed the phone into her jeans pocket so she wouldn't have to dig in her bag if it rang again. By the time she reached the bakery, she'd had another three dropped calls. Feeling slightly uneasy now, she put her phone on silent while she went into the bakery to choose a cake for the librarian. As she came out, she got the distinct feeling she was being watched. She started walking toward the library, constantly looking over her shoulder to see if she was being followed. There was no one there that she could see, but the shadows told her otherwise.

9

The Unraveling

Someone *was* following her; she knew it. She couldn't see them, but she could see their shadow ducking and weaving behind her, jerking out of sight every time she turned her head. Sophia was terrified and felt tears of fear pricking at her eyes. Abandoning the library visit, she decided that her safest course of action was to return home to her apartment. Once safely inside and the door securely locked, she could finally start strategizing her next move. She walked as quickly as she could without running, praying that whoever was following her wouldn't attack her in a public place in broad daylight. She clung tightly to that hope until she returned to her apartment, where she immediately locked the door and checked all the windows.

When an inspection of the apartment proved her to be the only occupant, Sophia started to doubt herself. She couldn't deny the stress she'd been under or the severe effect insomnia was having on her mental health. *Did I invent a mysterious imaginary stalker?* Perhaps the shadows she saw were simply trees and bushes, and her frazzled psyche chose to turn them into something more sinister. *Besides, who would want to follow me?* Sophia could only think of Hart, but she knew on some level that lurking in the shadows

79

wasn't his style. If he were trying to frighten her, he'd want to take credit for it.

Sophia made herself a cup of chamomile tea to soothe her nerves and contemplated what to do next. Her investigation into Jamie would have to wait for now; she had more pressing matters to deal with. Whether her stalker was imaginary or not, Sophia felt a real sense of danger. She couldn't stall any longer; she had to expose Hart and his connection to the murders before did anything to prevent her doing it. *Or worse, someone else gets killed.* Shuddering at the thought, Sophia drained her teacup, intending to head straight for the police station. But before she could do so, her phone buzzed with a message from the last person she wanted to hear from: Lucas Hart. Oh God, why hadn't she blocked his number? She decided to read the message anyway in case it contained more evidence she could take to the police, but the contents threw her off her stride:

Lucas: My dear Sophia, I really need to see you. Could you come to my office, please? X

The endearing tone and kiss at the end were so unlike Lucas that Sophia had to check the sender's number several times to convince herself he was really the sender. It was so unexpected that all her previous affection for him bubbled to the surface again before she could firmly push them back down. *What does he want?* They hadn't parted on bad terms after their last meeting, but if he sensed her reluctance to engage with him in his manipulation games, he would perhaps deduce that she was on to him. In which case, it may very well have been him following her earlier, not to mention making all the dropped calls she'd received. *If he suspects me, is it safe to meet with him?*

Sophia reasoned that no harm could come to her on a bustling university campus in the middle of the day, so she should go and hear what he had to say. But although she was reluctant to admit it to herself, there was another reason why she wanted to see him. Deep down in her heart, she still hoped she was wrong about him and that there was an innocent reason for his involvement in the murders. After all that had passed between them, he deserved the chance to put his side across before she went to the police. With some trepidation, she shouldered her bag and made her way across town to the campus, where Lucas was waiting for her in his office.

He looked up from his desk as she walked through the door. "Sophia! I'm so glad you came," he greeted her, jumping up to kiss both her cheeks. She was stunned by his uncharacteristically affectionate behavior.

"Well, you said you wanted to see me," she mumbled as she tried to gather her thoughts. "But there's something I think you should know first."

Hart's eyes narrowed slightly, and he stepped back from her. "Really? What would that be?" he asked.

Sophia took a deep breath and continued. "I know that you explained that Julie was your student, and that's how you learned about Laura's murder. But I also found a notebook in your desk containing information about Emily Warren and an experiment of yours she was involved in. That could have been passed off as a coincidence as well until I discovered that Emily's boyfriend, Robert, was one of your students. Plus, you've been behaving so strangely since Emily's murder with all the talk of manipulation games. There's information about both you and the murders missing from the university library. Finally, someone's been stalking me, and I think it could be you. You know I've worked out your involvement, and you're trying to intimidate me into silence."

Hart's face took on an expression Sophia had never seen before. He smiled widely, but his eyes were cold, calculating ice chips. "Okay," he said calmly. "Tell me what it is you think you've worked out."

Sophia sensed the danger, but she was in too deeply to back out now. "I think you've been manipulating your students for years and using them in your twisted experiments. And when their loved ones start becoming suspicious, you silence them."

Hart began to clap his hands slowly. Sophia's eyes widened. This was not the response she'd anticipated.

"Bravo, my dear, bravo, although I'm surprised it took you this long. I'm also slightly disappointed that you're not entirely correct, though. I expected more from you, to be honest."

Sophia gazed at him, speechless.

"I left all the clues in plain sight for you, but you've only scratched the surface. You may think you've uncovered the truth but underestimated the depth of your own involvement."

"What do you mean?" Sophia gasped.

"Well, let's look at the facts, shall we?" Hart slipped into full professor mode. "You've uncovered connections between the victims, their loved ones, and myself, but you've automatically assumed I'm the perpetrator. Correct?"

"Yes," whispered Sophia.

"Wrong!" said Hart gleefully. "I never got my hands dirty at all. I've never needed to."

"I... I don't understand," stammered Sophia. "Are you saying that you're not the killer?"

"Correct!" answered Hart. "You got that part totally wrong. You were right about one thing, though—I do use my students for experiments."

His use of the present tense sent shock waves of terror through Sophia's mind.

"This is how it happened," Hart continued calmly. "The study of manipulation and how it's used for criminal activity has plateaued. I could take it so much further, but I have been thwarted at every turn due to so-called "ethical issues." Honestly, I don't know what the world is coming to."

He shook his head at Sophia as though they were having a perfectly normal conversation.

"Anyway, being the first psychologist to push the boundaries of manipulation and prove its limitless possibilities with human behavior would propel me into the stratosphere of fortune and fame where I belong. Where I deserve to be."

At this point, Hart's eyes glazed over, and Sophia realized with dread that his brilliant mind had completely broken free from reality.

"But no one would fund my research or publish my findings, so I continued to experiment alone. I manipulated my students, yes, and used them to choose my victims. But I didn't commit the murders. They did."

Sophia opened her mouth to scream, but no sound emerged.

Hart put a finger to his lips and then carried on. "Yes, that's right. I manipulated my students to the point they would murder a loved one in cold blood just because I willed them to do it. Remarkable!" He was sounding increasingly unhinged.

"But why were they never caught?" gasped Sophia, unable to stop the tears streaming down her face.

"Yes, I'm surprised you never picked up on that," Hart purred. "You're such a clever girl, Sophia. Let's see if you can work it out now. The clue lies with the boyfriends. Laura's and Emily's," he added helpfully.

Sophia looked blank.

Hart tutted. "Come now, Sophia. What did Laura's boyfriend's father do for a living?"

"He was a senator," said Sophia, confused.

"Correct!" boomed Hart. "And Robert's father?"

"A university dean," whispered Sophia.

"Two out of two!" Hart looked very pleased with himself. "Both were very prominent members of society who wouldn't want their offspring's name to be tarnished with a murder charge. Have you got it yet?"

"They made the investigations disappear." Sophia was so scared and miserable that she thought she might vomit.

"Exactly! I knew you would get there in the end. As soon as I met you and discovered the subject of your thesis, I knew I wanted to work with you. It helped that I find you incredibly attractive, though. That part was real."

Sophia wanted to flee but was frozen on the spot. There was one question burning in her mind.

"You mentioned my involvement," she asked Hart. "Am I to be the next victim? Is that why you let me know all this because I'll be dead before I can expose you to the police?"

"Oh, Sophia," breathed Hart. "For such a clever girl, you can certainly get things wrong sometimes. Think about it. You're my student, and my students aren't the victims. Not only does it not fit the pattern, but it also links directly to me, which won't do at all. Try again."

"I was the next killer?" Sophia's eyes were out on stalks.

"Future tense, Sophia, not past. You will be the next killer. But you won't be alone. I've proved beyond doubt now how one per-son can be manipulated so much that they will brutally murder someone close to them on my whim, and honestly, it's not that hard to do. The results from my experiments are spreading fast on the dark web, and it won't be long before someone else steals my ideas and tries to claim the glory for themselves. I've got to go bigger.

"How about I manipulate two students simultaneously in different parts of the country, one in person and one remotely, to kill someone close to them both at the same time and in the same place? I don't know of anyone else who possesses the skill required to do that except for yours truly."

There was silence for a moment as Hart basked in his own perceived glory, and Sophia considered the ramifications of what she'd just heard.

"Jamie!" she suddenly gasped as the realization hit her.

"There, you did it! I always knew you would, and my judgment is never wrong." Hart was like an overstimulated cat, playing mercilessly with his prey before devouring it. "Exactly! And the victim?"

Sophia had to clamp her eyes shut tightly to stop the room from spinning.

"It was never going to be you, Sophia. Not everything's about you, you know. It was always about your mother."

Sophia grabbed Hart's desk to prevent herself from keeling over. "No!" she gasped. "You can't!"

"I can, and I will," he said firmly. "All the wheels are in motion, and I couldn't stop it now, even if I wanted to. Jamie's further along in the experiment than you, so don't even think about going to the police. One word from me, and your mother will be dead in minutes."

"NO!" Sophia cried helplessly.

"Oh, come now," said Hart reasonably, as if he hadn't just threatened to have her parent murdered. "Surely you can see how great this could work out for you? Think about your thesis—you'll be famous overnight."

"Or behind bars." Sophia was so hysterical she didn't know what she was saying.

"I don't think so," said Hart mildly. "Remind me, what does Jamie's father do for a living again?"

"He's the Chief of Police," said Sophia miserably.

"That's right," said Hart. "Also, Jamie is a very successful businessman in his own right, thanks to me. I'm sure he could make it disappear by himself if he had to. Or else..." He trailed off.

"What?" asked Sophia, although she didn't really want to know.

"We could always pin it all on him. And the other murders, too. We could make it look as though he was obsessed with you since your schooldays, and he murdered your mother and tried to frame you for the other two murders in some sort of twisted revenge for you not wanting him."

"It wasn't like that," Sophia could barely speak through her sobs. "He cheated on me, that's why I left him. But I had a breakdown and ended up institutionalized because of it."

"You think I don't know that?" retorted Hart. "It's your history of mental instability that makes you the perfect subject for this experiment. Your mind is more... susceptible... than others. But the truth doesn't matter here. With Jamie out of the picture and no murders to answer for, we could be together, Sophia, and continue this great work I've started. Together as a couple."

Sophia knew then that she had to make a run for it. Hart had completely lost the plot, and she'd be lucky to leave his office alive. She had to focus on saving her mother, and she couldn't do that if she was dead herself. That thought caused Sophia to experience an adrenaline rush, and she used the extra strength it gave her to push Hart back with all her might. She was no match for him physically, but he was caught off guard and staggered backward. That was all the time she needed to spin around and out of his office into the corridor, where there were too many witnesses for him to harm her.

She ran out of Emerson Hall as fast as possible and didn't stop until she was outside the university grounds. He didn't seem to be following her, so she stopped briefly to catch her breath. The next thing she knew, someone had grabbed her from behind and was holding her tightly by her wrists. Sophia struggled to free herself, and as she did so, she could tell by the slight stature of her assailant that it wasn't Hart. Sophia also sensed a lack of physical strength in her attacker and fought as hard as possible. But suddenly, she felt a sharp pain in her wrist, and then she fell to the ground, her legs buckling under her. She looked up, her vision blurring, and saw a figure standing over her, although she couldn't determine who it was. "What do you want?" she managed to gasp weakly.

The assailant didn't answer but stepped closer to Sophia instead, blocking out the sun like an ominous cloud. As the darkness closed in around her, Sophia's last conscious thought was that she might have been safer staying in Hart's office. At least she knew what she was dealing with in there. This was something different, although she had a strange feeling that the two events were somehow connected.

10

The Final Game

When Sophia's eyes fluttered open, the first sensation she experienced was a searing pain in her head. Slowly coming to her senses, she began to take in her surroundings. Although the room was dimly lit, she could make out some faint shadows dancing on the walls. She tried to move, but her body felt heavy, and her limbs were sluggish. Panic surged through her as she started to piece together what had happened and remembered being attacked by the unknown assailant.

"Ah, Sophia," taunted a familiar voice. "Welcome back to the land of the living!"

As Sophia tried to turn toward the voice, she realized her wrists and ankles were restrained. Twisting her head despite the pain, she saw Hart standing over her, his expression cold and mocking. "Where am I?" she croaked, her voice barely a whisper.

"You're in my world now," Hart replied, and she could see his eyes gleaming with a sinister light. "Congratulations on making it through to the final stage of our game."

Sophia's mind raced as she tried to understand what had happened to her. The room itself didn't hold many clues to where she was as it contained very little, but beyond Hart, she thought she could make out a large shape lying immobile on the floor. "This doesn't make sense," she rasped. "I know it wasn't you who attacked me."

"Oh, don't worry about her; she's served her purpose and is of no further use to us," said Hart dismissively.

Her? Sophie tried to remember what had happened when she was attacked. She remembered the mysterious figure standing over her and then... "Julie!" she exclaimed. "It was Julie who attacked me. But why did she bring me here to you? And where is she now?" Then, the large shape behind Hart caught her eye again, and the terrible realization hit her. "Is that...?"

"Like I said, she served her purpose," Hart interrupted. "She drugged you and brought you here, but that's the end of her involvement. This is all about us."

The shock heightened Sophia's senses, and she became aware that she was lying on the floor of an unfamiliar room with her ankles bound together and her wrists handcuffed to some sort of cabinet.

"What do you want from me?" she asked, unable to keep the fear and anger from her voice.

Hart chuckled mirthlessly, the sound sending an icy chill through Sophia's spine. "I want to see how far you will go, Sophia," he said softly. "You've done so well in the game so far. Will you make it to the finish line?" He chuckled again.

"You're insane," said Sophia, her heart pounding painfully in her ribcage.

"On the contrary, my dear," purred Hart, enjoying himself now. "My sanity has never been in question. Yours, however..." He shook his head and tutted. "How did you enjoy your little sojourn in the asylum when you had your breakdown? I expect it was a good test of your character."

Sophia tried to remain calm, but Hart's cruel words and erratic behavior were making her tremble from head to toe.

"How strong are you, Sophia?" Hart continued. "How much more can you endure? In all my experiments, you have been the best subject to date, a testament to your psychological resilience. Your determination, your intelligence... You've impressed me in so many ways."

Hart leered at her, and Sophia felt nauseous.

"You know you won't get away with this," she told him. "People will come looking for me."

"Perhaps, eventually," Hart admitted. "But for now, I have Jamie telling your mom that you've gone on a study retreat, which was also what you told the university in your voicemail."

"What voicemail?"

"The one that Julie left on your behalf. She actually proved herself to be quite useful in the end. Who would have thought? She abducted you and brought you here, so there are no ties to me. She's been driven mad with guilt since I manipulated her into murdering her sister, but I still have evidence that proves she did it. Therefore, it was easy to convince her to continue doing my bidding under threat of exposure to her parents and the police. Unfortunately, her weak mind was the undoing of her, and she kept threatening suicide unless I released her from my clutches. I grew tired of her threats and let her perform this last task for me before putting her out of her misery myself. Her parents and the police will assume it was suicide, though; I've made certain of that."

Sophia couldn't allow herself to think about whatever was lying on the floor behind Hart. She knew that she needed to remain calm if she had any chance of outsmarting him, but the minute she started processing what had happened to poor Julie, she knew she would crack.

"So," he continued relentlessly, "by the time anyone starts looking for you, it will be too late. The game will be over, and the results will be in."

"I don't know what twisted experiment you've made me part of," said Sophia, trying unsuccessfully to insert some bravado into her voice. "But I do know that you've underestimated me. I'm not as susceptible as you think."

"We'll see." Hart's face remained impassive. "It's time for you to prove to me that you're as strong-minded as you think you are."

Sophia's thoughts weren't coherent enough to formulate a plan, so she tried to buy herself some time instead. "So, what do you think you're going to make me do?"

Hart smiled at her coldly, his eyes like chips of sapphire. "Do you really think I don't know what you're trying to do? Fine, I'll play along. Nobody has managed to outwit me so far, Sophia, but who knows, you may be the first! This may well be my final experiment, as your investigations have raised some red flags. So, I've upped the stakes. You're going to kill Jamie for me, Sophia. Unfortunately, you'll be the prime suspect, as it's well-documented that you had a nervous breakdown when he cheated on you and you broke up. But it's a risk you're going to take; otherwise, I'll make him kill your mom. Do you understand now?"

"I'll never kill for you," Sophia whispered, almost incoherent with terror.

"Really?" Hart snapped and stepped toward her. Sophia closed her eyes and braced herself, thinking that he intended to harm her. Instead, he removed something from a drawer in the cabinet to which she was handcuffed. He held it up to the light, and Sophia could see that it was a small vial. "You ruined my idea of you and

Jamie working in collaboration, so you owe me. Do you know what this is, Sophia?" he asked with a lilt of dark amusement in his voice.

Sophia shook her head, causing the room to spin. She clamped her eyes firmly closed to stop it.

"It's a neurotoxin—a very potent one at that. One drop is enough to cause excruciating pain, followed by paralysis and then death. This is what Jamie will be armed with when he reaches your mother's house..." Hart looked at his watch. "Very soon. That's what he'll inject her with unless you reach him first and kill him. It's as simple as that."

Sophia forced herself to open her eyes and look at Hart. "Why are you doing this?" she asked.

Hart's eyes gleamed with sinister satisfaction. "Because I can," he replied, "I want to know how far I can push you through manipulation, how much psychological torture you can endure. It's the ultimate test, Sophia. The final game."

Sophia knew then she was dealing with a madman and that time was running out for her to escape either her own death or her mother's. "I had real feelings for you," she sobbed convincingly, again trying to buy herself a little time, "and I thought you felt the same."

Hart leaned in close to her, and his voice was a low whisper. "You've been such a fascinating subject, Sophia, in so many ways. It doesn't have to end like this. You could join me in my work. Just think of what we could accomplish as a team! So, will you join me? Or will you face the consequences? Because if you don't join me, I can't let you live, whichever choice you make. You'll be too much of a liability."

Sophia was incredulous. "I would never join you. If you think for one minute that I would, you're delusional."

"Disappointing, Sophia," Hart said, stepping away from her again with the harsh gleam back in his eyes. I thought you were the one person intelligent enough to realize that's the only satisfactory conclusion this game can reach. Otherwise, your fate is guaranteed, and you'll have two deaths on your conscience—Jamie's and your mom's."

Sophia looked at him sharply.

"Oh yes, I plan on killing them both, whoever you decide to save. Perhaps you'd like to watch?"

She turned her head to the side and prayed that she wouldn't black out. She had the beginnings of a plan in her mind. *I just need a few more seconds to think...*

Hart was still talking. "Did you ever consider what would happen to you once you'd completed your graduate degree?"

For a split second, Sophia was reminded of the Professor Hart she had fallen for, her respected and trusted mentor. But the memory was brief.

He continued, "You'll be thrust out into the real world, forced to compete with lesser scientists for fame and fortune that should be yours for the asking. You're so beautiful and clever, Sophia, even though you don't see it. Yours is the only scientific brain I've encountered that's even a patch on mine. If we combined our skills, we'd be in a class of our own. Think of the research we could write about, the theories and hypotheses we could develop... We'd earn our place in the history books in no time. Who knows, perhaps it could even be a legacy we could leave to our children. Because yes, Sophia, I do have feelings for you, and I can see us having a fantastic future together, both professionally and personally. What do you think?"

Sophia thought death might actually be preferable to the picture he had just painted. However, his extended monologue had given her the thinking time she needed. Yes, his actions had proved him to be clinically insane. But his ability as a professor had never been in doubt, and she had the benefit of his teachings on her side—his own theories on the power of manipulation, which she now intended to use against him. She took a deep breath and tried to calm her racing heart. This was going to take every ounce of grit she possessed. "Okay," she said finally, trying to keep her voice steady. "I'm listening."

Hart looked triumphant. "I knew you'd see reason eventually," he said softly. "You're far too intelligent to let that amazing scientific brain go to waste. Working with me is the only way you will use it to its full potential. And you can't deny the chemistry between us, Sophia. I know you felt it as much as I did that night in my office."

"Yes, I did." Sophia tried to sound seductive, although it was difficult with her teeth still chattering with fear. She knew, however, that for her plan to work, she'd have to pander to his narcissistic, Machiavellian, psychopathic ego. "I tried to fight it for ages. I never thought you'd look at me twice, with me being a grad student and you such a respected professor. But when you agreed to mentor me, and we started spending so much time together, it just grew and grew."

"And now?" he breathed, the lust in his eyes causing Sophia to doubt the wisdom of her plan.

"Well, I can't say I wasn't concerned when I learned about your experiments. But I was also intrigued—I guess that's why I wanted to learn more about them. I was too scared to ask you, so I researched them on my own. Okay, some may consider your methods unethical, but your results really got me thinking. No one has ever managed to fully harness the power of manipulation until now. You've almost perfected it. What does it feel like?"

"Let me show you." Hart's excitement was almost palpable. "Let me guide you, Sophia. Believe me, there's no other feeling in the world that can rival it. Think of all we could unlock by working together."

"Okay," she said quietly. "I'll join you."

Hart said nothing, but the triumph on his face only exacerbated Sophia's nausea. She nearly lost it completely when he leaned forward and hugged her, but she managed to hold herself together, remembering how high the stakes were in this game they were playing.

"I'll release you." Hart appeared to be talking to himself rather than Sophia. "We can start right now, this very night!"

"Mm-hmm. " While he worked on releasing her restraints, Sophia took a more detailed look at her surroundings, trying to identify anything she could use as a weapon. The room didn't yield much to satisfy her requirements, only the vial of neurotoxin on the cabinet that Hart had taunted her with only moments before. He had freed her wrists from the handcuffs with a key from his pocket and was now working on releasing the leather straps that bound her ankles.

Sophia wriggled her wrists, trying to get the blood circulating again. It was then that she noticed some surgical instruments on the cabinet along with the vial, including a syringe and a small scalpel. Just as Hart slipped the leather straps over her feet, Sophia seized her chance. Without giving herself time to think, she leaped up, grabbed the scalpel, and lunged at Hart. She intended to plunge it straight into his chest wall, but he was too quick for her and threw his arm in the way instead. Although the scalpel was small, it was incredibly sharp, and he started bleeding significantly from where it sliced through his skin.

"You, you..." Hart was incredulous as he stood there clutching his damaged arm.

Sophia was horrified and began frantically looking around the room for a way out. Locating the door, she dashed toward it as fast as she could.

"You've made a huge mistake," she heard Hart roar at her. "You'll never recover from this. I'll make sure that you don't."

Sophia reached the door and tried the handle, relieved beyond belief when it turned. But her relief was short-lived as Hart reached her side in a few long strides. She gasped in terror as he grabbed her arm.

"Game over, Sophia," he growled, "and guess what? You lose. I'm going to kill you and watch you suffer a slow and painful death. And I'm going to film it and make sure your family and friends watch so they can suffer with you until the day they die."

Painful sobs wracked Sophia's body as she saw him produce a full syringe containing what she assumed to be the neurotoxin. She knew this was it—Hart was under the Dark Triad Influence, and she had pushed every boundary until he lost control. He would carry out his threats with no guilt or remorse. Wishing that she had time to say a proper goodbye to her mom, she closed her eyes and gasped as she felt a sharp pain in her side.

11

Resolutions

The only sign that Sophia was still alive was the pain raging through her body. Although her mind was foggy, she ascertained that she was no longer in the room where she had lost consciousness. Although it was as dimly lit as the first room where she had been held captive, it was smaller and contained no furniture she could make out. She was also pleasantly surprised to discover she wasn't restrained. Panic surged through her as she recalled what had happened between her and Hart. But she wasn't dead, so there was still hope she could turn things around and prevent Hart from claiming any more lives. Of course, that meant leaving this room and finding him, neither of which she was sure she could achieve in her weakened state. Still, she had come this far and wasn't prepared to go down without a fight.

Despite her positive self-talk, Sophia still winced when she heard footsteps approaching. She steeled herself, however, and prepared to face Hart for one final showdown, whatever the outcome might be. The door creaked open, and someone entered. But it wasn't Hart.

"Hello, Sophia."

"Julie!" Sophia gasped in surprise. "I thought you were dead! What are you doing here?" And then she remembered. "It was you who brought me here. You're working for him!"

Julie shook her head. "Not anymore," she said emphatically. "It's over."

"What do you mean?"

"I refuse to be his lab rat any longer, but I can't live with what I've done. Did you know he made me murder my sister?"

Sophia nodded sadly.

"After he made me bring you here, he injected me with the neurotoxin. I played dead, and he thought it had killed me. It very nearly has. I haven't got long left."

For the first time, Sophia noticed how Julie's face was drawn with pain and how every word and breath was an effort.

"But I needed to rescue you before it was too late. I can't let him kill you, too. I know saving you doesn't make up for what I've done, but at least it's a start, and it proves I'm not a totally terrible person."

"He's the terrible one, not you." Sophia's mind raced as she tried to think of a plan to save them both. "Where is he now?"

"Locked in the room where you were held before. He thought I was dead, and so he wasn't paying attention. That's when I made my move. I shoved past him and managed to drag you out before he even knew what hit him. The key... it was still in the lock outside, so I turned it and locked him inside. It won't hold him for long, but it should give you just enough time to get safe and call the police before he breaks free."

Sophia nodded, an idea taking root in her mind. "Where are we?" she asked.

"It's a disused office building in downtown Harefield. Earmarked for demolition, I think. Unfortunately, there's nothing to connect Hart with this place; he's made sure of that."

"Okay." Sophia spoke slowly to buy herself more time to think, although the way Julie was starting to slur her words told her they didn't have long left. "One more question. He injected me with the neurotoxin. How come I'm not dead? I don't feel as bad..." She stopped herself from finishing the sentence, which would have ended with "as you look."

"I knew he only had one more vial of the neurotoxin with him in that room. He's so arrogant that it never occurred to him that his plan wouldn't work. So, I swapped it for a sedative when he wasn't looking. He gave me some sedatives to use when I abducted you, but I didn't need them all. You were knocked out, so he thought the neurotoxin had worked. He was just about to drag you away somewhere when I overpowered him. Luckily, we were both near the door; otherwise, I'd never have been able to get us out."

These final words seemed to use the last of Julie's strength, and she looked around desperately for somewhere to sit. Of course, there was nowhere, so she slumped against the wall and slid to the floor, her eyes wild with pain.

"Stay with me, Julie," whispered Sophia frantically. "You saved my life, and now I'm going to save yours."

Julie made one final effort to speak. Her voice was so faint that Sophia had to get down on her knees and crawl beside her to hear what she was saying.

"It's too late for me. I don't want to be saved. Save yourself and stop Hart. Do it for me. Please." Julie reached out for her as her head lolled to one side.

Sophia immediately tried to feel for a pulse, but there was nothing. Hart had claimed another victim. Tears streamed down her face, but she couldn't allow her the luxury of grief. That would come later. Right now, her priority was finding Hart. Facing him again was the last thing she wanted to do, but she knew she had to if she wanted to stop her ex-boyfriend from killing her mom on his command.

With one last look at Julie's lifeless body, Sophia made her way to the office door. "Okay," she whispered. "Goodbye, Julie." She hoped she stayed alive to make good on her promise. As she left the room, Sophia realized she didn't have a clue which office Hart was locked in. "Oh, well, I'll have to try them all," she thought, hoping the building wasn't too big. As it happened, she was in luck. She thought she heard faint sounds from the office on the left, which had a large key protruding from the lock. Now that Sophia realized how far the neurotoxin had infiltrated Julie's bloodstream before she saved her, it made sense that she wouldn't have had the energy to drag her very far. Sophia vowed to herself that she wouldn't let her mom suffer the same painful fate. The thought bolstered her courage, and she turned the key in the lock and pushed open the door.

Hart was in there with his back to her, bent over the cabinet, which he clung to with both hands.

"Hello, Lucas," she said softly.

He spun around to face her. "Sophia," he gasped. "What the…?"

"Yeah, I'm not dead," she admitted. "Sorry about that. There was a little mix-up with the vials. So, the game's not over yet, Lucas. I thought we could play another round."

He narrowed his eyes warily, looking like a tiger ready to pounce. "What do you mean?"

Sophia knew that rather than becoming helpless prey, she would have to play the part of a bigger, meaner predator to save her mom. "I mean, you were right. I guess I've always known it, deep down."

"Right about what?" he asked suspiciously. "I'm not falling for that ploy again. You're a dead woman walking, but I'll hear you out."

"What I meant was, you've proven your point." Sophia tried to stay calm, despite his threats. "You've shown me the depths of human resilience, the power of psychological manipulation. I see it now; I understand. It's a formidable skill to have."

Hart looked unconvinced. "And?" he inquired.

"You've always been one step ahead of me in this game, right?" It was a rhetorical question. "I mean, it was to be expected. You're the professor, and I'm the student, after all."

Emboldened by the glimmer of satisfaction in his eyes that Hart couldn't suppress, Sophia started walking toward him. She reached the cabinet and walked to the other side, forcing him to turn and face her. "I want to push the boundaries of psychological research even further."

"With me? How do you expect me to believe that after the stunt you just pulled?"

Sophia thought about poor Julie lying dead in the room next door and steadied herself to play her trump card. "I've been thinking about everything you taught me," she explained, trying to sound contemplative. "About the nature of control and how the mind can be both a prison and a key. You were right about all of it."

Hart's vanity took over, and he couldn't hide his intrigue.

"What conclusions have you drawn?" he asked as if Sophia was merely his student and not his potential murder victim.

Sophia's heartbeat started to accelerate. "I've concluded," she began, struggling to keep her voice steady, "that the greatest strength lies in unpredictability. In making the unexpected move."

"What are you getting at?"

Sophia leaned across the cabinet, so her face was only inches away from his. "You've underestimated me," she said. "You claim to know everything, but you don't. You're not as in control as you think."

Hart's expression darkened again, and his eyes flashed with anger. "I knew it," he said, "you're bluffing."

"Am I?" Sophia challenged him without dropping his gaze. "You've taught me well, Lucas. You taught me how to manipulate and how to control. And now it's time to put those skills to practical use."

Moving swiftly, Sophia bent down and retrieved the discarded handcuffs she'd concealed under her foot. Without missing a beat, she swung them at Hart's head with all her might and watched him slump to the ground with a thud, a trickle of blood running down his forehead. She quickly grabbed the leather straps that had formerly held her ankles and were conveniently now lying on the floor beside Hart. She grabbed his wrists and lashed them to the cabinet while Hart mumbled incoherently. Only when she was sure he was fully restrained did she slap his face with the full force of her wrath.

The shock jolted him back into consciousness, although he was deathly pale and still bleeding.

"You've lost, Lucas," she told him, enunciating clearly so there was no ambiguity in her words. You're not the master manipulator anymore. I've stolen your crown."

"Why?" he was barely able to formulate the word.

"Because I can. And now I'm going to kill you. Unless you agree to my terms, of course."

"How?" One-syllable questions seemed to be the limit of his capability.

Sophia regarded him curiously for a moment and then reached into her pocket and produced the vial of neurotoxin that she had retrieved from Julie in her dying moments. The one Julie had swapped with a sedative to save Sophia's life.

Hart obviously recognized it, and Sophia saw fear in his eyes for the first time. She pressed her advantage. "Now, the offer of a partnership still stands. But as equals, not mentor and student. I want equal credit for the work we do."

"Fine." Hart started looking hopeful.

"Good. All you have to do is to tell Jamie to stay away from my mother, and if any harm comes to her, you'll kill him yourself. Will you do that?"

Hart nodded weakly and tried to gesture with his head to the pocket of his tweed jacket. Sophia understood and reached into the pocket, although being so close to him again made her want to hurl. She extracted a cell phone—obviously a burner by its age and limited functionality. She loosened his wrists just enough to give him the hand mobility required to text and then pressed the syringe to his neck.

"Go on," she said softly and watched him give the order, a wave of sadness washing over her when she realized she still knew Jamie's phone number by heart. It wasn't until the reply came back—

Jamie: Roger that, Boss. J

—that she removed the syringe from Hart's neck and stepped back.

"Are you going to untie me now?" Hart's tone was almost pleading, and Sophia fought against the thrill of pleasure it sent through her body.

"Oh, Lucas," she shook her head at him. "Did you really think I would? Surely you must know that you taught me better than that?" Sophia did a victory lap in her head when she saw the resigned look on his face. "Now, I really should kill you, but that would make me a murderer like you, and I won't give you the satisfaction. Instead, for the sake of Laura, Emily, Julie, and whoever else's lives you ruined, I'm going to turn you in to the police, and you can face justice for what you've done. Not to mention public disgrace. Goodbye, Lucas." And without looking at him again, she straightened her back and walked out the door.

But just as she was closing it behind her, she noticed the door next to it—the entrance to the office where Julie had drawn her last breath. And it unleashed something in Sophia. Something that had been dormant but now exploded from her like molten lava from a volcano. She turned around and re-entered the room she'd just left. Without saying a word, she walked straight over to Hart and plunged the vial of neurotoxin deep into his neck, pushing the plunger on the syringe as far as it would go. Then, she calmly withdrew the syringe and walked out again without a word, ignoring Hart's screams as she found the exit to the building and made her way to the police station in central Harefield.

12

New Beginnings

The sun was setting, casting a warm, golden glow over the town as Sophia sat by the window of her old bedroom at her mom's house. Although it had been six months since she had fled Hart's clutches and left him for dead, her psychological scars ran so deep it still felt as though it had happened yesterday.

"Thanks, Mom." Sophia turned and smiled at her mother, who had quietly entered the room after knocking and placed a mug of coffee on Sophia's desk.

Sophia's mom returned her daughter's smile and briefly placed her hand on her shoulder before leaving Sophia alone again with her thoughts. Over the past few months, she had learned that Sophia liked calmness and predictability—anything outside the norm was likely to trigger flashbacks to her trauma. So, she mostly left her daughter to her own devices, but delivering the 11 a.m. coffee had become a habit.

Sophia sipped her coffee, trying to find solace in the simple ritual. Outside, everything was continuing as usual. People took their kids to school, went to work, and walked their dogs—all oblivious to the troubled woman who sat by her bedroom window, watching them while turmoil roiled within her. She was a survivor, as her therapist repeatedly pointed out. But although she had survived, she was far from whole. Her understated beauty remained intact; the long, chestnut brown hair still waved softly around her shoulders, her lashes were still long and dark, and her fair complexion was still complemented by the light dusting of freckles across her nose and cheeks. But there were subtle differences. Her clear green eyes, still intense and observant, now reflected an unmistakable wariness. Her demeanor was even more serious, and her experiences had left her more guarded than ever.

Forcing her gaze away from the window, she glanced at the stack of papers accumulating on her desk. She had finally submitted her thesis, having been granted an extension by Harefield University, and was now preparing for her new role as a criminal psychologist. But alongside the reams of police reports and psych evaluations she had been studying lay the beginnings of the memoir she had started writing at her therapist's suggestion. Sophia found it cathartic to process the chaos that had upended her life.

She still suffered from chilling night terrors. Every night, she relived those harrowing moments with Hart. She would wake up in a cold sweat with her heart racing and the fear gripping her chest like a vice, thinking that he was standing at the end of her bed, watching her because he had disappeared.

After she had left that disused office building with Hart's screams echoing in her mind, she had gone straight to Harefield police station. She revealed all that she had discovered about Hart and his twisted experiments that had left multiple people dead, culminating in him kidnapping her and threatening to murder both her and her mother. The only fact she omitted was that she had administered a fatal dose of neurotoxin to him before she left. She had made sure that she disposed of the vial so that no forensic evidence remained that could link her to his murder. She simply assumed that the police would find him dead, the cause of which would remain a mystery.

Her ex-boyfriend, Jamie, corroborated her story when the police questioned him about his involvement. Unfortunately, during their investigations, they uncovered some dubious business transactions, and Jamie was now cooling his heels in the county jail, awaiting trial for fraud and larceny.

But when the police arrived to arrest Hart, they found the office building deserted apart from a deceased female, who was later identified as Julie. Against all odds, Hart had somehow managed to escape his restraints and flee into the night. This was despite the deadly venom coursing through his bloodstream, although, of course, the detectives weren't aware of that. He was now officially listed as a missing person and a wanted man. Consequently, Sophia lived in constant fear that he was coming for her. Everyone around her was sympathetic—she had survived a traumatizing ordeal, and the perpetrator had escaped, so it was natural she would fear recrimination. But no one had any idea just how deep-rooted her fear had become, exacerbated by the guilt she carried for attempting to kill him.

During the day, Sophia kept herself busy as a distraction from the dark thoughts that threatened to consume her. She took long walks, visited museums, and studied tirelessly for her new role, immersing herself in books and research. But no matter how hard she tried, she couldn't escape the ever-present memories lurking in the night's shadows.

Her therapist, Dr. Rachel Peacock, was a trauma recovery specialist. Their sessions were intense, often reducing Sophia to tears. Still, Sophia appreciated that they helped her navigate the labyrinth of her mind and confront the demons that haunted her.

"You've survived an imaginable trauma," Rachel repeatedly told her. "You know yourself that it's going to take a while to recover from that. Give yourself time to heal. You're strong, Sophia. Stronger than you realize."

"Don't let your fear control you." Hart's words constantly echoed in her brain, giving her no respite from the fear and guilt their relationship had left her with. Unable to share the fact that she had tried to kill him with anyone, she felt that it ate away at her conscience night and day. It was like she was walking on a tightrope, constantly on edge, with it just being a matter of time before the next disaster struck. Her friends and family, especially her mom, reached out with support and encouragement. But Sophia's defenses were firmly in place, and she struggled to let them in. Trust was such a fragile thing, and Sophia's trust in herself and others had been shattered. Therefore, as hard as she tried, she struggled to rebuild those connections. She became insular as a form of self-preservation, afraid of being hurt again.

Her mom was patient and caring, and her friends were persistent, especially her high school best friend, Amy. Amy had moved to the city, but called Sophia daily, and eventually, Sophia could let her guard down enough to engage with her. They spoke for hours, catching up on lost time and sharing stories and memories from their childhood. It was a small step, but it felt like a progression to Sophia, who finally realized she wasn't alone in the world. She had family and friends who cared about her and wanted to help if only she'd let them.

But as hope started slowly creeping back into her life again, it was cruelly banished to the shadows once more by a ring at the doorbell. Her mom was out, and Sophia was working on her memoir in her bedroom. She was initially frustrated as she was desperate to finish the chapter, but frustration was slowly replaced by anxiety as she realized she wasn't expecting anyone. She was relieved when she opened the door to find nobody there, but that relief turned to dread when she saw a small envelope on the ground. There was no sender's name or return address—just her own name and address in neat, precise, and chillingly recognizable handwriting.

Her hands shook as she bent down to retrieve it. She returned to her bedroom and laid the envelope on her desk, staring at it while dread washed over her in waves. She knew exactly who had sent it and also knew she should take it directly to the police without opening it. But she couldn't.

She tore open the envelope with trembling fingers and pulled out a single sheet of paper. She read the contents with an escalating chill in her spine.

My Dearest Sophia,

I truly hope this letter finds you well. You will now be aware that I am, despite your best efforts, still alive. I'm sure you will have many questions, and I look forward to answering them all in time. I confess that I still think of you often, especially our night of passion. You were, without a doubt, my most promising student and fascinating subject. You may believe you escaped from me as I escaped from you. The truth, however, is that a connection such as ours is unbreakable. Our paths will cross again, I promise you.

Until then, I remain.
Forever yours,
L.

Sophia struggled to catch her breath as she re-read the letter that confirmed her worst fears. It wasn't over, and even attempting to kill him apparently hadn't dampened the fire of his obsession. She crumpled the letter in her hand and threw it to the floor, trying to breathe deeply and concentrate on her surroundings, as her therapist had taught her. But she was overwhelmed by emotions—fear, anger, confusion... and something else she couldn't quite place. *How does he know where I live? Is he out there now, watching me?* She quickly ran to her window and pulled the blinds before frantically running through the house and double-locking all the doors.

She felt a bit calmer then and ran through some of the relaxation techniques she'd worked on with Rachel. Arming herself with a soothing cup of chamomile tea, she returned to her bedroom and opened the blinds. A barrage of thoughts raced through her head as she stared out at the town below. She had come so far and was within touching distance of reclaiming her life. But now Hart had cast his shadow once again, and she was reminded of the darkness that still lingered inside her. Because, despite everything, Hart was right. She still felt a lingering connection, a part of her that couldn't wholly sever their bond. She was actually relieved he was alive—not because it meant she wasn't a murderer, but for other reasons she didn't care to dwell on.

Sipping her chamomile tea to steady herself, she vowed she wouldn't let Hart control her again. She wasn't that person anymore—there was no way she would allow him to dictate her future. But as much as she tried to deny it, part of her couldn't relinquish the twisted intimacy they had shared. It was a bond forged in the crucible of fear and manipulation, and it had become as much of a part of her as the heart that pumped blood through her body.

Her thoughts drifted to the times they had spent together, good and bad. He had pushed her to her limits but, in doing so, had awakened a strength and resilience she wasn't aware she possessed. Their connection was dark and complex, and it both repelled and fascinated her in equal measure.

Almost against her own will, she smoothed out the crumpled letter on her desk and re-read it. Her common sense told her she should hate him and everything he stood for. She should take the letter to the police and let them find him. *But you can't,* her inner voice reminded her. *Because then they'll know that you tried to kill him.* She could run—far away where he could never find her. *But is that what you really want?* her inner voice taunted her again. *No, it isn't.* Because a part of her would always be drawn to him, they understood each other in a way no one else could.

Just then, she heard her mother return home, so she quickly pushed the letter under her mattress and tried to look as if nothing had happened. She spent the rest of the day in her room, gazing at the wall while a fierce battle played out between her head and her heart.

Sophia didn't expect sleep to come easily that night. She lay in her bed, eyes open wide, staring into the darkness. She knew she had to stay in control and write her own narrative if she didn't want to spiral into the depths of insanity again. So, what were her options? Yes, she could create a new life for herself, but she knew she'd never rid herself of Hart's presence, looming like a dark cloud on the horizon. She knew their story wasn't over but had suppressed it so deeply that it was no longer at the forefront of her thoughts—until she had received that letter. Oh, Lucas was good; she had to hand it to him. He had waited until just the right moment to remind her they had unanswered questions and unfinished business.

Turning on the light above her bed, she fished her journal from the drawer in her bedside cabinet and flipped to a blank page. She began to write, her thoughts flowing freely. She poured everything onto those pages: all her fears, hopes, and dreams. As she did so, a plan began to take shape. Somehow, writing everything down helped her make sense of the chaos and allowed her to see the path she had to follow clearly.

Starting a new journey would be daunting, with challenges and obstacles to overcome. But she was ready to face them and take on whatever came her way. She had survived Hart's twisted games and would continue to thrive, whatever the future may bring. Because if Hart had taught her anything, it was not to let her fear control her.

Sophia closed her journal and set it aside, finally finding the peace she'd been craving. She didn't have all the answers yet, but she had a direction and a destination. Everything else would follow, one step at a time.

The night was still and quiet as Sophia settled back down on her pillow. She closed her eyes and drifted into a peaceful sleep, knowing that her next chapter would be written on her own terms. She was master of her own destiny now. She was finally free.

13

Epilogue

With only the shadows cast by the small desk lamp for company, he stared at the letter he had just finished writing. It had taken a while to compose as each word was carefully chosen—a calculated move in an ongoing game. He'd given her some time, let her think she was free. Now, he was eager to explore the next chapter of their twisted journey.

Acknowledgments

Writing this book has been a journey filled with twists and turns. I want to express my deepest gratitude to everyone who played a role in bringing this project to life.

To my family and friends—thank you for your unwavering support, encouragement, and patience as I immersed myself in the world of this story. Your belief in me has been my constant source of strength.

A special thanks to my editor, for your keen insights and dedication in helping me shape this book. Your attention to detail and guidance have been invaluable.

To my readers, new and returning, I owe you a heartfelt thank you. Your support inspires me to continue writing stories that resonate with you, and I hope this book captivates you as much as it did me.

Thank you all for being part of this incredible journey.

ABOUT THE AUTHOR

Filiz Behaettin is a best-selling author, speaker, and freelance writer with a talent for captivating readers across various genres. Born and raised in Melbourne, Australia, with Turkish Cypriot heritage, Filiz brings a rich cultural background and unique perspective to her work.

She is also the author of '*Elevate: The Practical Guide to Living Your Best Life and Succeeding*', a self-development book that has resonated with readers worldwide, and the popular children's series '*Henry the Strange Bee*', known for its enchanting storytelling.

Now venturing into psychological thrillers, Filiz's latest book takes readers into a world of suspense, intrigue, and complex characters, showcasing her versatility as a writer.

To learn more about her work and upcoming projects, visit www.filizbauthor.com.